best buddies

sisters of the heart

soul sister

friends forever

kindred spirits

sister-friends

SISTERCHICKS
do the Hula!

pals for life

girlfriends

chum

W0009677

confidante

gal pals

true blue

ally

From one sisterchick to another...

"Robin Jones Gunn is the perfect tour guide for this joy-filled Hawaiian adventure. You'll feel the sand between your toes, taste sweet pineapple juice, see amazing rainbows—all without having to put on a bathing suit! Your travel partners, two turning-forty chicks, will feel like old friends the minute you hit the beach. Funny, touching, and true to life, *Sisterchicks* will have you doing the hula (and loving it!) by the last page. Grab your grass skirt, girlfriend—this is one trip you don't want to miss!"
—LIZ CURTIS HIGGS, BESTSELLING AUTHOR OF BOOKENDS

"In real-life, Robin Gunn is my very own special sister-chick! Her books capture the warmth and humor that mark our friendship—and that keep readers hooked until the last page. Sit back and enjoy!"—KAREN KINGSBURY, BESTSELLING AUTHOR OF THE REDEMPTION SERIES

"The beauty of Robin's graceful writing many times brought laughter and tears. *Sisterchicks on the Loose* was so wonderful, I didn't think she could top it, but *Sisterchicks Do the Hula* is Robin's best work yet. I can't wait for the next book!"—DOING THE HULA IN OREGON

"What a vacation. Made me want to fly the coop with my sisterchick!"—KRISTINA

"Sisterchicks Do the Hula is one more step in my spiritual journey of awakening. The depth of the book embraced me with lessons on living in the unforced rhythm of grace. The last time I visited Hawaii, I was a *haole*. The next time I visit, it will be with a whole new understanding of *aloha.*"
— ELIZABETH

"I picked up *Sisterchicks Do the Hula* and absolutely could not put it down! It made me feel like I was wiggling my toes in the warm sands of Waikiki Beach. It made me laugh out loud and cry a couple of times. But most of all it made me want to head out to North Dakota, grab my best girl-friend, Sherry, and hop a flight to Honolulu to see what kind of sisterchick adventure we could have together!"
—KATHLEEN

"I will never hear the word *aloha* the same. No longer a trendy island greeting, it's the essence of welcome. So is the story of Hope and Laurie. As the island breeze blew its aloha, God's breath was blessing me with each page. Robin welcomed me to enjoy another wonderful story of fun, friendship, and aloha!"—MARGARET

PRAISE FOR *Sisterchicks on the Loose*

"Deliciously fun! The feel-good book of the season!"
—Patsy Clairmont, bestselling author of GOD USES CRACKED
POTS and STARDUST ON MY PILLOW

"This is a fun tale that feels like Lucy and Ethel taking Europe
in the 1990s, yet each one remembers why they were and
still are best friends while renewing their faith in God. The
key to the tale is the message that plenty of life remains to
enjoy for the over-forty crowd. Readers, especially middle
age, will appreciate these super Sisterchicks on the Loose."
—MIDWEST BOOK REVIEW

"*Sisterchicks on the Loose* is fast-paced and was a great read.
I have personally gotten a lot out of this book and think
that all women, young and old, should read it."—FICTION
GUIDE ON ABOUT.COM

"While *Sisterchicks on the Loose* is 'chick lit' for Christian
women, a spiritual message is carefully woven through
without preaching but with great impact. I highly recommend *Sisterchicks on the Loose*. It is a fun read-in-one-sitting
book. It'll make you smile."—THE WORD ON ROMANCE

"Look out, Finland! Look out, England! Look out, good ol'
U.S. of A.! It's *Sisterchicks on the Loose!* If Robin Jones
Gunn's title doesn't grab you, the content will grab any
over-forty female gazing nervously at the second half of
her life…. Gunn's bouncy, conversational style and steady
servings of insight feed the soul and warm the heart. Over
forty? The best is yet to come!"
—*ROMANTIC TIMES* MAGAZINE

a sisterchick™ novel

SISTERCHICKS
do the Hula!

ROBIN JONES GUNN

Multnomah® Publishers *Sisters, Oregon*

SISTERCHICKS DO THE HULA
published by Multnomah Publishers, Inc.

© 2003 by Robin's Ink, LLC
International Standard Book Number: 1-59052-226-5
Sisterchicks is a trademark of Multnomah Publishers, Inc.

Cover image of women by Bill Cannon Studio
Background cover image by Jon Arnold Images/Alamy

Unless otherwise indicated, Scripture quotations are from:
The Message by Eugene H. Peterson
© 1993, 1994, 1995, 1996, 2000, 2001, 2002
Used by permission of NavPress Publishing Group
All rights reserved.
Other Scripture is from:
The Holy Bible, (NKJV)
© 1984 by Thomas Nelson, Inc.

Multnomah is a trademark of Multnomah Publishers, Inc. and is registered in the U.S. Patent and Trademark Office. The colophon is a trademark of Multnomah Publishers, Inc.

Printed in the United States of America

For information:
MULTNOMAH PUBLISHERS, INC. • P.O. BOX 1720 • SISTERS, OR 97759

Library of Congress Cataloging-in-Publication Data

Gunn, Robin Jones, 1955-
  Sisterchicks do the hula / by Robin Jones Gunn.
      p. cm.
  ISBN 1-59052-226-5 (pbk.)
  1. Female friendship—Fiction. 2. Women—Hawaii—Fiction. 3. Women travelers—Fiction. 4. Hawaii—Fiction. I. Title.

  PS3557.U4866S56 2004
  813'.54—dc22

                                        2003020681

05 06 07 08 09 10—10 9 8 7 6 5

OTHER BOOKS BY ROBIN JONES GUNN

SISTERCHICK NOVELS
Sisterchicks on the Loose
Sisterchicks Do the Hula

THE GLENBROOKE SERIES
Secrets
Whispers
Echoes
Sunsets
Clouds
Waterfalls
Woodlands
Wildflowers

GIFT BOOKS
Tea at Glenbrooke
Mothering by Heart
Gentle Passages

www.sisterchicks.com • www.robingunn.com

For Cindy, who flapped the red hibiscus bedspread over the lanai, and for Carrie, who did all the driving around Honolulu and got only one ticket. You two are the best prayer pals a sisterchick could ever ask for.

And for Janet, Julee, Kathleen, and Lisa,
who gently made this a better story
with their editorial expertise.

For the Daughters of Hawaii, Calabash Cousins,
and staff at the Mission Houses Museum.
You made me feel welcome with your gracious *aloha. Mahalo.*

"Are you tired? Worn out? Burned out on religion?
Come to me. Get away with me and you'll recover your life.
I'll show you how to take a real rest.
Walk with me and work with me—watch how I do it.
Learn the unforced rhythms of grace."

MATTHEW 11:28-29

Prologue

$\mathcal{L}$aurie came up with the idea to go to Hawai'i. Both times.

The first time she made the suggestion was in 1983, when we were sophomores at UC Santa Barbara. I was up to my eyebrows in shattered bits of my heart when I burst into our dorm room to blurt out the news: My engagement was off. While I had been busy trying on bridal gowns and ordering invitations for the June 19 wedding, my fiancé was leaving work early to smooch with some seventeen-year-old cinnamon twist who worked at Taco Bell.

Laurie saw it coming, but to her everlasting credit, she didn't try to collect my heart's fragments and glue them back together. Instead, she administered a steady supply of tissues for my big, globby tears and listened patiently until I had no more words to spit at her.

"Hope, listen to me," she said firmly. "You're going be okay. Better, actually."

I said something about how the only thing that would make me better would be some serious chocolate. So we proceeded to the vending machine at the end of our hall and ceremoniously inserted our precious laundry quarters until all the Oreos and Reese's Pieces were ours. Returning to the room, we ate every last dot and crumb while sitting cross-legged on Laurie's sheepskin rug.

"I think we should go somewhere on June 19," Laurie said. "Someplace exotic."

"Why?"

"Because you need a fresh start. A new dream. Something wonderful to look forward to. Where should we go?"

The only place I wanted to go was a dark cave where I could hibernate for six months.

"I have an idea." Laurie rose to her feet. She fluttered her arms about to the right and then the left while awkwardly swishing her hips. "What do you think?"

"I think you need hula lessons," I said flatly.

"Exactly! I *do* need hula lessons. And so do you. That's why we should go to Hawai'i. On June 19. Just the two of us."

I let the word *Hawai'i* plant itself in my ravaged soul like a lone tiki torch flickering in the midst of all the smoke and ashes. *Hawai'i.*

All we needed was some money.

Laurie and I spent spring break in Napa Valley working at the restaurant Laurie's parents owned. We hoped for many generous tippers, but it turned out there was only one. Gabriel Giordani.

Before my eyes, Laurie fell in love with this struggling artist who came to the café every day with his two daughters. His wife had passed away a few years earlier, and all the locals loved to gossip about Gabe and his paint-splattered jeans. Laurie gave them something to really gossip about our last morning there, when she kissed Gabe on the mouth, right in front of the café window.

She and I were about three miles down the road when Laurie said, "You know what, Hope? I'm going to marry that man."

I studied her profile and solemnly said, "I know."

I also knew that on June 19 Laurie and I would not be flying to Honolulu. Somehow, it was okay.

Many years later, when my husband and I saw one of Gabriel's paintings in a restaurant, I told Darren that, looking back on that season of my life, I realized I didn't need the actual trip to Hawai'i as much as I had needed the possibility of such an adventure. That was what Laurie gave me—she dared me to dream when I wanted to die.

Darren said I should get back in touch with her because true friends like that are hard to come by.

"I know," I said. "But Gabe is practically famous now. They've probably moved to an estate. She might not remember me."

"She'll remember you."

"I don't know if the phone number I have is right anymore."

"You won't know until you dial it and see."

But what would I say? *I miss you, Laurie. By any chance, do you still have the key to the back door of my heart? Because I have yet to make a duplicate and give it to another friend.*

No. I wouldn't call Laurie or write her. The season of our friendship had passed.

Then, as only God can, He surprised me. I think He prompted Laurie to call out of the blue just to prove that He knows me by heart. He knows what I need even when I'm too timid or belligerent to ask for it. Laurie and I had an unfinished dream. Neither of us had yet learned to do the hula.

One

The day Laurie called me she was in New York.

I was in the garage, mopping up psychedelic puddles of Rocket Pops. Our ancient freezer had coughed its last icy breath sometime during the night, and the entire summer supply of Little League frozen confections was forced to seek alternate accommodations. Unfortunately, the Popsicles tried this on their own and met with disaster.

"Gabe has meetings all afternoon," Laurie said, after I recovered from the shock of hearing her voice in the middle of my mess. "I know it's last minute, but I'd love to drive up to see you."

"Are you sure?"

"Yes, very sure. If it's not too inconvenient."

I warned her about the Popsicle massacre. "And it'll take you a couple of hours. Are you sure you want to drive?"

"Yes, I love to drive. Remember?"

I smiled. Yes, I remembered. Laurie had a passion for the open road. "Are you going to rent a convertible?"

"You know it! Now don't go to any trouble."

I hung up the phone, rinsed my permanently cherry-scented mop, and frantically began cleaning the rest of my humble abode like Tigger on steroids.

When Laurie pulled into the driveway three hours later, she emerged from a black convertible sports car and smoothed her straight blond hair. Back in college her hair was as brown as mine.

She looked taller than I remembered. Maybe because I was feeling rather small at the moment, hiding behind the living room curtains, spying on her and wishing I had done all the laundry last night so the dryer wasn't making that thunking noise in the background.

Laurie adjusted the collar on her crisp white sleeveless shirt and pulled off her sunglasses. For one paralyzing moment, I couldn't imagine what we would talk about.

I opened the front door, and miraculously all time and differences evaporated. We hugged and starting to talk over the top of each other's sentences, as if we were back in our dorm room. All that was missing were the Oreos and Reese's Pieces.

We talked nonstop. I only remember one part of the marathon conversation, which was when Darren returned from the park with our three boys. They looked hot and frazzled and ready to be home. I couldn't believe the afternoon was gone.

The words that sprang from my mouth were, "But we're not done yet."

Laurie started to cry sniffly little tears. An untrained ear might think Laurie was simply trying not to sneeze, but I knew she was crying. Laurie leaked and squeaked. I slushed and gushed. We knew this about each other.

"You're right," Laurie said. "You and I are not done yet, and I have a feeling we never will be." She blinked quickly and tried to smile for Darren's benefit.

Laurie stayed long enough for pizza. She promised to call me the next day from her hotel. We talked for two hours. I called her the next week. She called me the week after that. I called her the next and so on.

"Think of it this way," I told Darren, when I showed him the phone bill a few months after Laurie and I reconnected our coast-to-coast friendship. "It's cheaper than therapy."

"What do you two talk about?" he asked.

"Everything."

"Like what?"

I shrugged and listed topics Laurie and I had covered during the past week. "Varicose veins. New ways to fix chicken. The ozone layer. Coffee prices. Fabric softener. You know, life stuff."

"But you don't drink coffee."

I looked at him and thought, *How come men don't get this? It's so basic.*

"Laurie and I need to stay connected. It keeps me sane when I talk to her every week."

"For eighty-seven minutes about chicken recipes and fabric softener?"

"If that's how long it takes, yes. Sometimes we talk longer if we discuss our hair or our hormones."

Darren left the room shaking his head.

The next time Laurie called, Darren answered the phone. He talked to her for a few minutes before Laurie put Gabe on so that our husbands could meet. The two men talked for almost five minutes, which surprised me.

That night, when Darren climbed into bed, I said, "What did you and Gabe talk about for so long?"

Darren looked at me with that smirk of his. "Oh, you know, the usual. Fabric softener. Hormones."

I laughed so hard I got giggle tears all over my pillow. I was the happiest I'd been in a long time. I couldn't explain where all the joy came from. I already had a great life with a wonderful husband and three healthy sons. But now I had Laurie again, and she was filling up a place in my life that had been empty for a long time.

Laurie and Gabe started coming to Connecticut every fall for a week to get away from the frazzled pace of their lives. They loved the New England autumn colors, and we loved seeing them. That became our annual get-together for six years in a row.

Then last August, Laurie called. "Gabe can't manage a free week this fall for our New England getaway. I'm so disappointed."

"Oh," I moaned. "Are you sure? Not even for a quick week-end?"

"It doesn't look like it."

"I'm so sad, Laurie."

"I know. But I was thinking about taking a *Roman Holiday* instead."

"You want to go to Italy?"

"No, *Roman Holiday,* the movie. You know, with Audrey Hepburn. Remember how she played a princess who ran away for a few days to escape the pressures of royalty?"

"Are you saying you're tired of being rich and famous?"

"Gabe is the one who is rich and famous. I'm just the one who is tired. But not too tired to run away. Seriously, Hope, I need to get out of here. I'm going crazy. I'm busier than ever because I keep filling my calendar with stuff, but I'm not passionate about anything. I'm just trying to be productive. What I need is to get away and think things through. With all the girls out of the house now, I'm not sure who I am or what I'm supposed to be about."

"Getting away will help you figure that out?"

"I think so. I hope so. I can't focus on anything for very long here at home. I keep getting interrupted. That's why I'm ready to declare a Roman Holiday around here and run away for a few days."

"So, if you don't want to go to Italy and you both can't come here, where do you want to go?"

"Hawai'i."

In a carefully guarded corner of my heart, the original tiki torch that had flickered faithfully for almost two decades spiked into a flame. I didn't let Laurie hear the blaze in my voice. "Hawai'i, huh?"

"Yes, Hawai'i. Don't you think it's about time the two of us got our little hula hips over to the islands?" Laurie's voice had definitely elevated. "Just the two of us, like we planned back in college. What do you think, Hope?"

"I think…" A gust of reality all but extinguished the flame. I was the one with the balloon payment coming up on our mortgage and three teenage sons headed for college. Nothing woven into the fabric of my DNA had ever allowed me to say yes to spending a large chunk of money on myself. "I think I'll have to think about it."

"I knew you'd say that. Don't say no too quickly. Run it past your honey when he's in a good mood, then call me back. Tell him you're being kidnapped by a runaway princess and you'll bring him back a case of macadamia nuts."

"Oh, yeah, that ought to win him right over."

"I'm serious about this, Hope. I really need something to look forward to. I need to go someplace where not one single person will ask me to do some favor for them because I supposedly have all this free time in my life now."

That afternoon I scuttled off to the video store like a dieter sneaking into the bakery aisle of the grocery store. I never took breaks during the day to watch TV or movies, but I rented *Roman Holiday* and watched it by myself. As the credits ran, I thought, *Laurie is right. She needs to do this. I need to do this. We need to go to Hawai'i.*

The next morning I called Laurie. "I have only one request. Could we rent scooters like Audrey Hepburn did and go darting about in the Honolulu traffic?"

"I take it you're warming up to the idea?"

"Warmed, toasted, broiled, and fried. I'm all for it, Laurie."

"Are you sure?"

"Yes, very sure. I have all green lights on my end. Darren said we have enough frequent flyer points in his account to cash in for my round-trip airfare."

"So when do you want to go?"

"I had an idea about that, too. Why don't we go the end of January since our birthdays are only a few days apart? We'll both be turning forty, you know."

"As if you need to remind me."

"Don't you think it would be memorable to turn forty in Hawai'i?"

"Hope, you are a genius. Should I start checking into hotels?"

"I'm already ahead of you. Open your e-mail. I just sent you some options."

Before the day was over, we had booked our flights, selected our hotel room, and printed out a list of recommended restaurants in the greater Honolulu area. Twenty years earlier the plans required much more effort.

We e-mailed and called each other frequently over the next

few weeks. Laurie made me laugh. Every time she called she sounded like a jubilant nine-year-old planning her own surprise birthday party. The guest list for this party was limited to just the two of us, but the potential activities included horseback riding on the beach, snorkeling, sailing, taking a sunset dinner cruise, parasailing, lots of fruity tropical beverages with little umbrellas, and a big luau. Laurie was determined to celebrate our entrance to midlife with pineapple pizzazz.

However, before our bags were packed, a little stowaway had quietly added her name to the guest list.

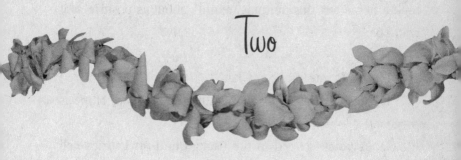

Two

On Thanksgiving Day, two months before our big birthday bash, Laurie called me as she and Gabe were driving to San Francisco.

"I'm trying to picture your home right now," she said. "Tell me if this is right. The dining room table is set with your grandmother's china, you've plopped an iced cranberry in each crystal goblet, and a garland of maple leaves is strung over the fireplace."

"You've got it," I said. "The guys are watching football and..." I paused and then decided to see if Laurie could decode my secret message. "The-turkey-is-in-the-oven."

"Are you saying that...?"

"Yep."

"Hope!"

"I couldn't wait for my doctor's appointment on Monday. I

took a home test this morning, and it's about as positive as it could be."

"Hope!"

"I know. Is this insane or what?"

"It's wonderful. Really. Congratulations! Gabe, Hope is pregnant!"

Gabe's voice echoed in the background on Laurie's cell phone. I could picture the two of them in their cashmere sweaters, settled in the leather seats of Gabe's Jaguar, roaring down the freeway headed for their oldest daughter's apartment.

"What did Gabe just say?"

"He said you're trying to make our trip more of an adventure by bringing a little extra baggage."

"Darren and I are still in shock."

"Have you told the boys yet?" Laurie asked.

"No, we're trying to decide if we should tell them at dinner or wait until later."

"Oh, tell them at dinner. It will make for a Thanksgiving memory like no other."

"I suppose you're right."

"How are you feeling, Hope?"

"Great. And listen, Darren and I already talked about it, and this does not change the plans for January. You and I are still going to Hawai'i."

"Are you sure?"

"Yes, very sure. If my calculations are correct, I'll only be into my fourth month in January. No one will even know I'm pregnant. I'll probably just look chubby."

"Oh, right. That's doubtful. With your long torso, you've always managed to hide any extra pounds that came along. You probably won't even be showing by then."

I stood to the side and smoothed my knit top over my midriff, trying to evaluate my shape in the oven door's reflection. Was it my imagination, or did I show a little already?

"Hope, listen, if you start to get morning sickness, or you're too uncomfortable, or concerned about the baby for any reason, we'll postpone the trip for another time."

"When? Our fiftieth birthdays? No, this is definitely the time for us to go. After this little pumpkin shows up, I have a feeling I won't be going anywhere for a long time."

"Okay," Laurie said. "But remember, I'm open to adjustments, if necessary. Let me know how it goes when you tell the boys."

That afternoon, when our family gathered around the dining room table, Darren prayed, thanking God for all He had given us over the years. After the hearty "amens," I lifted my head and noticed the exquisite way the autumn sunshine came pouring through the window, infusing the whole room with an amber glow. Glittering dust particles, caught up in a silent dance, swirled above the wooden floor. Every brass picture frame on the mantle sparkled. I couldn't have asked for a more golden moment to make the glad announcement to our sons.

I glanced at Darren. He gave me a wink and a nod, and I proclaimed that I was thankful for the baby, the baby that was growing inside me, the baby that would, Lord willing, be with us at this table next Thanksgiving.

The boys put down their forks and stared. Our sixteen-year-old blurted out, "Mom, you're kidding, right?"

"No, I'm not kidding. We're going to have a baby."

"Why? I mean…you guys! What were you thinking?"

Darren and I looked at each other.

"Man, this is kind of embarrassing for us, you know."

"Wait a minute," Darren said firmly. "We're a family here. We're in this together. Your mother and I are very happy about the baby, and you boys should be, too."

They didn't look convinced so Darren leaned forward and said, "Every child is a gift from God. It's not up to any of us to choose when we come into this world or when we go out. Your number one objective is to support your mother in this. Got it? Come on, I'm counting on you. All of you."

Our boys managed to stand as gentlemen and line up to give me a kiss on the cheek.

Mitchell, our oldest, said, "Sorry if we didn't seem very supportive. I think you'll make a great mom."

"Oh, you think so, do you?"

Thirteen-year-old Blake said, "Yeah, you've done a pretty good job with us. The new kid will probably turn out okay."

I tried to hide my smile.

Blake's expression turned to a scowl. "He's not going to share my room, is he?"

"We'll figure all that out later," Darren said, passing a bowl of mashed potatoes. "Come on, let's eat." No one had to offer food to our boys twice.

A week before Christmas, Darren went with me to the doctor for all the usual scans and tests. We found out that "the new kid" would be arriving much earlier than I originally had predicted. According to the doctor's calculations, the baby would arrive not in June but mid-April. That startling information didn't sink in right away because we also found out we were having a girl. And for that bit of news, I couldn't stop smiling.

Emilee Rose had been alive in my imagination long before she showed up, tucked snugly beneath my heart. The first two times I was pregnant, I was sure I was having a girl. By the time I was pregnant with our third son, I had resigned myself to accept that Darren and I were breeding our own football team. This time around I hadn't dared to dream for a girl, and yet here she was—my Emilee Rose. At last!

In every way, I was delighted to be "with child," as we celebrated Christmas and read about Mary wrapping her newborn babe in swaddling cloths and laying Him in a manger. All of life seemed to be miraculous and breathtakingly beautiful.

Then, on a Saturday afternoon in January, I snapped.

In five days Laurie and I were scheduled to meet up in Honolulu. What triggered my meltdown was an ordinary UPS box that arrived on my doorstep in the snow. Inside was my maternity bathing suit.

Blithely carrying the box upstairs, I drew the curtains,

closed the bedroom door, and peeled off layers of warm clothes. Relieved that the back-ordered item had arrived in time, I wiggled my way into the new swimsuit, slowly turned toward the mirror on the back of the bedroom door, and took in the sight of my blessed belly wrapped in swaddling aqua blue spandex.

First the front view. Then the side. Other side. Twisting my head over my shoulder, I got a glimpse of the backside. Then quickly returned to the front view.

I was shocked! Completely shocked!

The woman in the mirror shook her head at me. *"You're not considering going out in public wearing that, are you?"*

"Yes?" I answered with a woeful sigh. "Although, I didn't think it would look like this on me."

"Oh, really? And just what did you think it would look like on you?"

"Well, not like this."

For months I had been riding high on the "blessed-art-thou-among-women" cloud. I considered it a privilege to carry this baby. I told myself I was participating in a calling that was higher than fashion and charm. Who cares about beauty? The truth was, my body was nurturing new life.

However, truth and beauty had crashed head-on in my bedroom mirror.

"I like this shade of blue," I declared, trying to be positive.

"Yeah? Well, from where I'm standing, that shade of blue does not appear to be too fond of you, sweetheart."

"Maybe I could return this one and order the black one instead."

"Right, because everyone knows that black is always so much more slimming."

"There was that black one with the little pleated skirt…"

"Okay, yeah, there you go. Because nothing says dainty like Shamu in a tutu."

"Hey!" I turned away and covered my belly as if to protect Emilee's ears from this brazen woman. "You don't have to be rude about it!"

"Look who's talking."

I glared over my shoulder at the mannerless minx and found I couldn't say anything. I could only stare at her. At myself. At what I had become. How did this happen?

How could it be that my two dreams had intersected this way? Innocent little Emilee Rose was my dream baby come true. A trip to Hawai'i with Laurie was a dream that had waited patiently for two decades to come true.

But someone had taken my two best dreams and poured them into a single test tube when I wasn't looking. Now the churning, foaming result bubbled over the top and ended up larger-than-life in my bedroom mirror. There she stood, defying me to accept the truth.

I was old.

And I was not beautiful. How had those two facts escaped me in the bliss of being a middle-aged life bearer?

Fumbling my way out of the aqua swimsuit and trying to

stop the ridiculous flow of big, globby tears, I turned my back on the mirror and plunged into my roomiest maternity clothes. Leaning against the ruffled pillows that lined our bedroom window seat, I inched back the curtains and let the tears gush.

Outside, an icy January snowstorm was elbowing its way down the eastern seaboard, causing the limbs of our naked elm tree to shiver uncontrollably. Beside me was a tour book of Hawai'i. The cover showed shimmering white sand, pristine blue water, and a graceful palm tree stretching toward the ocean as if offering its hand for the waves to kiss. Beautiful people from all over the world came to bask in the sun and stroll along such exotic beaches in this island paradise.

I glanced sympathetically at the quivering elm tree out my window and tried to imagine slender tropical palms in full sunlight, swaying in the breeze, green and full of life.

"That's right. Think about the beautiful beaches, the sunshine, and all the fun you and Laurie are going to have."

I blew my nose and glanced at the mirror.

She was still there, delivering her sugary sass.

"Don't think of the other tourists—those twenty-year-old toothpicks in their bikinis, sauntering down the beach with their long, cellulite-free legs and their flat stomachs. Who cares that you'll be the only woman on the beach looking like a bright blue Easter egg on parade?"

I picked up a pillow, took aim, and...

The bedroom door swung open, forcing the mirror maven

into hiding. My hero entered with a tube of caulking in his hand. "There you are. You okay?"

I clutched the pillow to my middle and nodded.

Darren glanced out the window and then down at the tour book beside me. "I heard this storm is supposed to blow over by Monday. Should be clear sailing when you fly out on Wednesday morning."

"That's what I heard, too." My voice sounded surprisingly steady.

Darren stepped into our bathroom and proceeded to caulk the shower. "Hope, can you come here and tell me if this looks straight to you?"

I didn't need to go in there to see if his caulking line was straight. Darren's repairs were never straight. But they always worked. That's all that mattered to me.

"Looks good." I tilted my head ever so slightly so that the line along the base of the shower honestly did appear straight.

He glanced up from his kneeling position. With a tender pat on my belly, he said, "And you look good to me."

"Bahwaaaaah!" I burst into tears all over again.

"What's wrong? What did I say?" Darren was on his feet, trying to wrap both arms around me and draw me close. "Why are you crying?"

"How can I possibly look good to you? I'm pregnant! I'm really, really pregnant!"

"Of course you are. Why are you crying?"

"Because I'm going to Hawai'i!"

"Yes, you're going to Hawai'i. Come on now, pull yourself together."

I kept crying.

Darren looked frantic. He stepped back and fumbled for his roguish smirk. "So, is this a hormone thing?"

"No, it's not a hormone thing! I'm old, Darren! I'm old and pregnant, and I'm going to Hawai'i. Can you understand how that makes me feel?"

He could not.

How could I possibly expect my husband to understand all the bizarre things that happen to a woman in spirit and flesh when a friendly alien takes over her body? He still couldn't figure out why Laurie and I wanted to fly all the way to Hawai'i just to spend a week lounging around a pool, comparing underarm flab, when we could stay home and have the same conversation over the phone for a lot less money.

I took a deep breath. "You know what? I don't care what anyone says. These screaming purple stretch marks running up my biscuit-dough thighs are stripes of honor."

"Exactly."

"I earned every one of those zingers!"

"Of course you did, honey."

"I am a Mother, with a capital *M.*"

"Never doubted it for a moment."

"And everyone knows that aqua is the perfect motherhood color, even in the tropics."

"Especially in the tropics."

"Thank you, Darren."

"You're welcome."

What my husband had just observed was a 95 percent hormone-induced solar flare. But there was no way on this blue earth that I would reveal that scientific secret to him.

I concluded my little performance by clearing my throat and saying, "I think your caulking looks good. Very nice."

"Thanks. And I meant what I said. You look good to me, too."

"Thank you." I turned with my chin raised in valor and tried to glide gracefully out of the bathroom, my beach-ball belly exiting a full half a second before the rest of me.

Reaching for the much-debated swimsuit, I rolled it up and tucked it into the corner of my suitcase. Over my shoulder I could feel the mirror maven working up a good sass-and-slash comment. Before she had a chance to deliver it, I turned to face her full on. "Let's see now. One of us is stuck to a piece of particleboard, and one of us is going to Hawai'i. Any guesses as to which one you are?"

She didn't say a word. She knew her place. And I was about to find mine.

Three

The only advice the doctor gave me about the long plane ride was to drink plenty of water and to get up often to stretch my legs. Less than an hour into the flight, I realized the second part of his advice wasn't necessary. Getting up often was a natural by-product of drinking lots of water. I wondered if the high altitude was somehow compressing my bladder, making it impossible to hold more than a thimbleful of fluid for even twenty minutes. Fortunately, I had an aisle seat.

In between my treks to the back of the plane, I thumbed through a variety of magazines, snoozed off and on, and half-heartedly watched a movie that my sons had rented and enjoyed the week before but I had found uninteresting. After changing planes in Denver, I repeated the routine with the same turkey sandwich served in a box, the same movie, and the same magazine selection.

Just before the plane landed, I checked my purse for the

papers with the hotel information. Laurie's plane was to arrive two hours before mine. I guessed she already was at the hotel. I could picture her sashaying to the pool with a towel over her arm, sporting a new pair of classy sunglasses. The incognito princess. I couldn't wait to join her.

My suitcase was cruising the luggage belt when I descended on the escalator to baggage claim and joined the swarms of people. Several women in Hawaiian print shirts stood with orchid leis looped over their arms and held up small signs, each announcing the name of the tour company they worked for and the name of the party they were waiting to greet.

I wished one of their signs read *Montgomery* and that a garland of fresh flowers would be draped around my neck. Months earlier Laurie and I had discussed whether we should order a lei greeting at the airport since it was offered as an option with our hotel package. Laurie said it seemed too commercial, and if we walked around wearing leis, everyone would know we were tourists.

I felt differently now that I was here. Lots of people at baggage claim were wearing leis. Men and women. Not all of them appeared to be tourists.

One short woman with skin the texture of beef jerky was bedecked with four or five strands of flowers. They made her look beautiful. Honored. Beside her, two round-faced girls jittered and hopped, orbiting around their grandma like twin moons with hiccups.

"*Tutu*," one of them said, taking the old woman's hand. "Tutu, we have a new kitten."

So, a tutu *is a grandma or at least an elderly woman. My first Hawaiian word!*

Pulling my wheeled suitcase behind me, I stepped out of the air-conditioned building and into the tropical afternoon. I couldn't believe it still was daytime or that, in this place of light and warmth, the calendar read January.

A rush of warm, sweet air ruffled my hair and tickled my nose. A hint of diesel lingered but then came another brush of the fragrant breath. Closing my eyes and lifting my chin to the breeze, I filled my lungs. Something I'd read in one of the plane's magazines came back to me. The quote was from an essay Mark Twain had written long after he visited these islands in the mid-1800s. "In my nostrils still lives the breath of flowers that perished twenty years ago."

I smiled to think that the breath of flowers still rode on this island's winds nearly a century and a half after Twain stood here and breathed the fragrant air. Perhaps this island paradise hadn't been completely ruined with asphalt and skyscrapers as all the naysayers in Connecticut had insisted. The gentle, floral-laced winds still prevailed. Twin moons with pigtails still orbited around their tutus.

I liked Hawai'i already. Yes, I liked Hawai'i very much.

As I tried to decipher the various signs for the cabs and shuttle buses to find the one that would take me to my hotel, a large woman in a floral print uniform with a walkie-talkie in her hand stepped up to me and asked if I needed directions.

I pulled out my papers and showed her the name of the hotel.

"Oh, Kalamela Makai," the woman said. The Hawaiian words sounded like butter melting on her lips. She pointed to where a shuttle that serviced hotels would arrive soon and then offered to help with my suitcase.

"That's okay. I can get it," I said. "I need the exercise."

"Long plane ride?"

"Yes, very long."

To my surprise, she reached over and placed her hand on my stomach, as if I knew her and had invited her to pat the baby. Very few people touched my stomach. Ever.

"Take care," she said, as though it were a blessing. I found her gesture warming and strangely comforting.

I also found my layers of clothing warm but not at all comforting. As soon as I'd walked the twenty-five feet to the shuttle stop, I peeled down to the sleeveless shirt I had put on under my big sweater hours ago. What I really wanted to do was take off my shoes and socks and slide my swollen feet into my sandals. But the shuttle bus arrived.

I was the only one to board. In such privacy, I decided to try out my Hawaiian butter lips by saying the name of my hotel. "I'm going to the Kala-mela-maka," I said proudly.

He looked at me in the rearview mirror. "Kalamela Mauka?"

"Yes. Thank you."

The driver maneuvered through the traffic on the freeway while slow Hawaiian music floated from the overhead speakers. The view ahead of us was of a once-green slope now dotted with hundreds of houses. To the right, the vast ocean stretched out like a field of azure blue, dotted with occasional whitecaps that looked like wild daisies.

We inched down a side street, passing apartments with bicycles chained to the stairways and lines of laundry drying in the freeway fumes. A few blocks later, the cab turned toward the ocean, and we were enveloped by shadows cast by all the tall hotels on the right side of the road. I guessed the beach was just beyond the hotels but couldn't be certain. Not a wink of blue squeezed through the concrete forest.

Along the sidewalks, dozens of tourists swarmed like half-naked bees wearing their brightest stripes and trying to remember whose turn it was to go make some honey. I imagined that, despite being on vacation, they were so caught up in the city-ness of Honolulu that they hadn't figured out yet how to relax.

Laurie and I will not go scurrying around like that. We are going to relax.

A couple on a moped puttered past us on the left. The drone bee driving was nearly eclipsed by a buxom woman who clung to him. She wore a tight black tank top, short shorts, and a floppy red hibiscus flower behind her ear.

Aha! The queen bee is off on her Roman Holiday!

I couldn't wait to reach the hotel, kick off my shoes, pull

on a pair of shorts, and go find Laurie lounging by the pool.

The shuttle driver turned off the main road and down an alley. He stopped in front of a faded stucco building. It looked as dismal as the crowded apartments we had passed along the freeway.

"Is this it?"

"Kalamela Mauka," he sputtered. Nothing was soothing or buttery about the words the way he said them. He hoisted my suitcase and all but tossed it out the door. My feet were barely planted on the sidewalk when he pulled away, leaving me in a puff of exhaust. I held my breath and blinked in disbelief. This hotel looked very different on its website.

With unsure steps I entered the lobby. A single, downcast ficus tree adorned the small space along with two bamboo chairs covered in green and yellow checkered fabric. In front of me was an appointment window made of smoked glass that ran on a rusted metal track. I felt as if I'd been transported back in time to my orthodontist's office. Horrible memories pulled my chin down, sucking my saliva and taking my next breath from me. Instinctively, my teeth hurt.

"You checking in?" a tough voice called out.

I saw no one.

Moistening my lips and reflexively making sure my front teeth weren't clamped in braces, I stuttered, "Yes, I think so."

The smoked glass window slid open with a sandpapery-metal shriek. A red-haired woman with a patch over her left eye stuck her face out at me.

"You have a reservation?"

I nodded or quivered. At that moment it was difficult to distinguish between the two gestures. "It's under either Laurie Giordani or Hope Montgomery."

"You sure?" the one-eyed woman asked after checking her computer screen.

"Yes, we made the reservation on-line. Laurie should be here already."

"Nobody named Laurie has checked in. You sure you want the Kalamela Mauka and not the Kalamela Makai?"

"I'm not sure what you're asking me." I took a step back from the dreaded window. "I have the reservation here in my purse…"

I rummaged as the unsmiling woman leaned her neck way out, and with her good eye, took in a full view of me in my delicate condition.

Like a snapping turtle, she jerked her head in and slammed the window shut. *Screech!*

Appointment over.

Come back in two weeks and have your braces tightened.

Four

I stood as still as the drooping ficus anchored between the bamboo chairs. I couldn't get my feet to move even though a voice in my jet-lagged brain was shouting, "Run, Hope! Run for your life!"

Uneven footsteps came around the corner. It was she, the one-eyed, redheaded dental assistant. And she was pregnant. Very pregnant.

"So, when are you due?" she asked me as casually as if we were hanging out together in detention hall.

"Um, ah, the middle of April."

"I'm February 10. I don't know how I'm going to stand the wait. I'm crawling the walls around here."

I didn't check for nail scratches on the wallpaper. I believed her.

"Let's see your reservation."

I held out the paper.

43

She lifted the eye patch and appeared to use both eyes to read.

"Pinkeye," she said, flipping her pirate accessory back in place. "Itches like crazy. This is supposed to help with the irritation."

Again, I didn't need to check for scratches under the patch. I believed her.

"Yeah," she said, handing back the paper. "You're staying at the Makai. Those shuttle drivers. They don't care where they drop you. They get paid no matter if they deliver you to the right hotel or not. Here. Sit down. I'll call a cab for you."

I lowered myself onto one of the bamboo chairs and cautiously said, "I'm still not sure I understand. Are you saying two hotels have the same name?"

"Almost the same name. This is the Kalamela *Mauka*. *Mauka* is Hawaiian for 'toward the mountains.'"

"Oh, I see."

"You want to go to the Kalamela *Makai*. You know, *makai* as in 'toward the ocean.'"

"I didn't know that."

"How could you? You're a *haole*." She disappeared around the corner.

I wasn't sure what a haole was but guessed it wasn't a good thing.

Reaching into my purse I turned on my cell phone and saw that it was "searching for service."

"I know exactly how you feel," I muttered.

As soon as my phone managed to bounce a signal off its mother satellite, I listened to my missed message. It was from Laurie.

"Hope, I tried to reach you at home before you left this morning, but obviously I didn't succeed. Listen, I have a slight change in plans. I'm going to catch a later flight out of San Francisco. I think I should arrive close to seven o'clock tonight Hawaiian time. I'll call you later. Can't wait to see you! Bye."

I called Laurie back. No answer. In the background I could hear my maternity sister on the phone talking to the taxi service. I looked down at my tennis shoes and socks and felt very much like the "how-lee" or whatever that word was she had called me.

As soon as the beep sounded, I left a message for Laurie with my hand cupped over the cell phone, "Hey, Laurie, when you get to the airport, find a taxi and show the driver your reservation papers. Don't take the shuttle. And don't try to tell the driver the name of the hotel. Also, don't get out of the cab unless the hotel is right by the ocean and the lobby has more than one wilting ficus tree. Can't wait to see you. Bye."

A horn sounded out front.

"There's your ride."

That was fast! What kind of a racket do these shuttle drivers and cab drivers have going here?

"Thanks!" I called out to the shadow behind the closed window. I wondered if she was in on the scam. Shaking off my paranoia, I said, "Take care. I hope all goes well with your delivery."

"Yeah, same to you."

The Kalamela Makai hotel was only four blocks away, right on the water. The minute I walked into the spacious lobby and caught the scent of tropical flowers, I knew this hotel had to be the four-star one Laurie and I had viewed on-line. I checked in at the desk without any problems and went up to our room.

I was delighted to see that the room was just like the sample shown on the website. The bedspreads were a kitschy Hawaiian print in deep shades of cranberry red, dotted with huge white hibiscus flowers. The walls behind the beds were covered in wallpaper that was exactly the same print as the bedspreads. It created an optical illusion broken only by the white wicker headboards that matched the white wicker dresser and corner chair.

One thing was certain: When we woke every morning, Laurie and I would know we were in Hawai'i. We couldn't possibly wonder for a moment if we were in, say, Fresno or Toledo. We were definitely in Waikiki. Even though the hotel advertised that they recently had renovated all their rooms and given them the "retro" feel, it would take very little to convince me that, actually, nothing had changed since the seventies.

Kicking off my shoes, I decided to order a snack while waiting for Laurie. Room service recommended their island fruit salad, so I went with it. As an afterthought I added some cookies. White chocolate macadamia nut cookies. And a glass of milk for dunking.

I unpacked a few items and changed into a pair of shorts. Opening the sliding glass door, I stepped out onto the balcony, which the bellman had referred to as the *lanai*.

Through every pore of my weary body, I drank in the glorious view. A warm, welcoming breeze lifted the ends of my short, feathered hair and cooled the back of my neck. Far below lay a strip of caramel-colored sand dotted with hundreds of scantily dressed bodies. Bright beach umbrellas popped up at random intervals like wild toadstools.

Merrily rolling up to the edge of the sand came the gigantic Pacific Ocean, broader and bluer and more jovial than it had ever looked when I lived in Santa Barbara. A thin line of lacy foam, as white as the snow I'd left back in Connecticut, ran along the edge of the slowly uncurling waves. I stood for a long time, leaning on the railing, watching the ocean play tag with the tourists who traipsed along the shoreline and dared the wild, white wetness to touch them.

I held up my arm as shade from the lowering sun and scanned the endless stretch of blue sea, marveling at the mix of surfers and catamarans that skimmed across the water with elegant ease. I wanted to be out there with them.

That thought surprised me because it was a thought I would have had twenty years ago. The past few summers I'd become more of an umbrella lounger and shore stroller whenever we camped at the lake back home. I didn't want to be that sedate person on this trip. I realized that watching from the balcony wasn't satisfying enough. If all I wanted to do was observe such beauty, I could have stayed home and rented *South Pacific*.

South Pacific! *Ha! Now I'm starting to sound like Laurie, comparing life to cinema. I hope she comes before sunset so we can go down to the beach.*

I made myself comfy on the lanai with my cell phone beside me in anticipation of Laurie's call. The waves' rhythmic sound had a hypnotic effect. I easily could have fallen into a deep sleep had it not been for room service arriving with my snack.

The fruit salad was served inside half a pineapple with the spiky green leaves still attached to the top. I had no idea what the soft orange chunks of fruit were in the mixed salad. Mango, perhaps. Or papaya. I couldn't remember ever trying either of them. While I was growing up, our family never had extra money for exotic foods. Now I probably could buy mangoes or papayas at any well-stocked grocery store, but I never had been curious enough to spend money on something no one else in my household would be likely to try.

I loved being here, nestled in my little perch, savoring every bite of the fresh fruit. Breaking off a large chunk of cookie, I dunked it into the glass of milk and deposited the soggy sweetie into my mouth.

Oh, Laurie, you're missing all the good stuff. I can't wait for you to get here!

Looking up, I saw the beginning of a sunset that made me pray. That's the only way I can describe it. I felt so awed by what was happening before me that I put down the rest of my cookie and stood reverently with my hands pressed against my heart.

Wispy layers of orange and pink clouds trailed across the sky like silk ribbons edged with creamy white lace. The clouds appeared to be wrapping up the ocean as if it were a special gift. Fragrant winds soothed the hushed surface of the sea, covering the waters with what looked like lavender blue tissue paper.

My mouth opened as if trying to help my other senses take it all in. Two eyes alone weren't adequate portals for receiving such an ethereal sight.

I breathed in deeply as the sun, huge and round like a perfect orange, sank lower and lower until it was sliced in half at the edge of the world. Silently it slid—juice, rind, and all— over the side, into the unknown tomorrow.

A breeze came, different from the one I'd felt spinning around me when I first stepped out on the lanai. This twilight breeze seemed to come directly from the heavens. With invisible fingers the wind playfully tousled my hair once more and gently stroked my cheek. God was tucking in this pleasant isle for the night. I lifted my chin to receive His good-night caress.

I thought of something I'd read yesterday and went inside the room to find the book I had bought especially for this trip. It was a small copy of the book of Psalms in a contemporary version. I thought it would fit more easily in my suitcase than my large Bible and would give me a fresh look at familiar verses. At the moment I felt very close to the Creator. After all, He had just tucked me in for the night along with the rest of His exquisite creation.

Like any child who knows the morning will bring exciting surprises and long-anticipated gifts, I couldn't sleep. I flipped through the book until I found chapter 32 and read the part that had been rolling around in my memory:

> GOD's my island hideaway,
> keeps danger far from the shore,
> throws garlands of hosannas around my neck.

Reaching for a pen I underlined the words *garlands of hosannas*. Oh, I loved that phrase! It made me think of the fragrant leis I had longed for at the airport.

Laurie should have a lei to wear around her neck for her birthday tomorrow. Every woman who turns forty needs a garland of hosannas! I wonder if I can get one tonight in the gift shop? I could hide it in our little refrigerator and surprise her in the morning.

Feeling sneaky, I slipped out of the room and took the elevator. I was joined on the next floor down by a young Japanese couple who looked as if they were ready to go out on the town. I'm not sure if I imagined it, but they seemed to be taking turns staring at my belly and then staring at my white legs. I couldn't do much about the belly, but starting tomorrow morning, the goal was to toast my legs a nice shade of golden brown.

That reminded me. I needed to buy some suntan lotion at the gift shop. Funny thing, the grocery store at home in Connecticut seemed to be out of suntan products last week when I was shopping for my trip. However, they were having a special on snow shovels.

Snow shovels. Imagine.

I stepped out of the elevator with a grin so smug I felt positively snooty.

Five

Before I made it all the way through the lobby to the hotel gift shop, I had to go to the bathroom. I was convinced there was something scientific about elevation and compression and the effect gravity had on a pregnant woman's bladder. In the hotel rest room, I overheard two women talking.

"It's a wonderful luau," one of them said. "We went two nights ago and loved the show. They give you lots of food, but look out for the tiki punch. My husband had more than he should have, and when they asked for volunteers to do the hula, he was a little too eager to get up onstage."

The other woman laughed and said, "Been there, done that, lit the tiki torch."

I decided I would gather a bunch of event brochures in the lobby before going back to the room so Laurie and I could chart out our week. Originally she had a long list of activities that started with horseback riding on the beach. After Emilee joined the party, Laurie crossed that activity off as well as parasailing. Whenever we talked about specifics after that, Laurie said we would figure it out when we got here. She also said she would be content with a hammock strung between a couple of swaying palm trees, but I knew she was pulling back on my account. There was no reason she couldn't go parasailing or whatever she wanted without me. I wasn't going to let my condition hinder Laurie's adventure. Especially on her birthday.

The hotel gift shop had a nice selection of leis. They hung in a row beside the soft drinks in the refrigerated case. I chose one made from purple orchids and white tuberose because it seemed to shout, "Hosanna!" The others merely peeped a subdued, "Cheers."

Finding my way to the back of the store where the personal items were stocked, I scanned the choices of sun care products. As I reached for a tube of suntan lotion, I knocked over a bottle of coconut oil. Several boxes on the lower shelf became drenched with the fragrant, sticky stuff.

Tightening the lid on the coconut oil, I gathered up the ruined boxes and took them to the register, placing them on the counter along with the lei and the suntan lotion. Emilee did a little flutter, and I instinctively placed my hand on my rounded belly.

Just then I heard my name.

I turned to see Laurie, my Laurie, approaching the register

holding an orchid lei, fresh from the gift shop refrigerator.

"I can't believe you're here!" she squealed, as we threw our arms around each other. I'm afraid I squashed her when our middles collided.

Pulling back with an expression of unabashed surprise, she said, "Hope, look at you! I can't believe it! Look at you!"

The irony was that she wasn't actually looking at "me." She was gawking at Emilee's bunker.

"I told you I was big."

"No, no, you're not big at all." She quickly looked up at my face. "You're just…"

"All out front?" I suggested.

"Yes. Just, all…right there." Laurie started to move her hand toward me and then pulled back and used her itching fingers to tuck her professionally lightened blond hair behind her ear.

"It's okay." I grinned. "Go ahead. You can pat the baby, if you want."

Laurie cautiously pressed her palm across my tummy. "Hello, little Emilee Rose. It's your Auntie Laurie. How are you, sweet baby girl?"

Looking up at my smiling face, Laurie said, "You look great, Hope! Seriously, you look glowy."

"You look great, too."

"Oh, my hair came out way too light this time." Laurie brushed a few silky strands away from her face. "And I'm about ready to pop these contacts out. My eyes are so—"

"You ready to pay for this stuff?" The young man at the register obviously didn't understand how important it was for women to first do an inventory and evaluation of each other before they can turn their attention to spending money.

"Just this." Laurie held up the lei.

"You can put it back," I said. "I came down here to buy one for you."

"Are you kidding? Hope, I was buying this one for you. When I got off the plane and the greeters were there with all those beautiful leis looped over their arms, I—"

"I know! I wished we had ordered the lei greeting, too. I wanted to surprise you with this one for your birthday tomorrow."

"Hope, you're so good to me."

"Here." I reached for the garland of hosannas and tossed it over Laurie's neck. "Happy birthday, my friend."

Laurie teared up and started to leak and squeak as she placed the other lei over my neck and kissed me on the cheek. We acted like we were experts on Hawaiian greetings. "*Aloha*, my friend," she squeaked out.

"*Aloha!* Happy birthday."

"Happy birthday to you, too!" Laurie dabbed at her eyes and reached for her wallet. "Here, we better pay for these now. I've got it covered."

"No, I'm buying them. Both of them."

"You don't have to. Save your money, Hope."

"No, I'm getting some other stuff, so I'll buy the leis." I

pushed the money back into her wallet and turned to the young salesclerk. "You take Visa, don't you?"

He nodded.

"Don't use your Visa," Laurie said. "I have enough cash. Here."

"You know," the clerk said in a low voice, "it's none of my business, but I'm thinking you might be wasting your money."

"Excuse me?" we said in tandem.

"I'm just saying that if you want to save some money, I'm pretty sure all of these will come out positive. At least for you." He nodded toward my belly.

Laurie turned the three coconut-soaked boxes so we could read the packaging. "Hope, why are you buying three home pregnancy tests?"

I laughed so hard I had to go to the bathroom again.

"I spilled a bottle of suntan oil," I managed to finally say. "I was going to offer to pay for the damage."

Laurie cracked up.

"Oh, gotcha. Okay." The young man reached for the boxes and slid them under the counter. "Don't worry about it. You don't need to pay for these. And, hey, what I said earlier was just, you know, a little joke." He was turning red from the neck up.

"Don't worry. That's exactly how I took it." I handed him my Visa and tried very hard to keep my legs together and not look at Laurie's face. I knew if I started to laugh again my bladder wasn't going to cooperate any longer.

Bedecked with the chilled purple leis, Laurie and I trotted to the rest room and laughed some more.

"How's our room?" Laurie asked. "The bellman is probably up there waiting with my luggage."

"I like it. But you might want to think *Beach Blanket Bingo* when you walk in the door."

"Annette and Frankie." Laurie slipped into her movie trivia mode as we headed for the elevator. "Remember when they showed that one on the outdoor screen during orientation week our freshman year?"

I had forgotten.

"Are you hungry?" she asked. "I ate already, but I didn't know if you were waiting for me before you got something."

"No, I'm fine." I told her about the fruit salad and cookies and the incredible sunset. "Do you want to walk on the beach or unpack or what?"

"Part of me would love to go out on the beach, but part of me wants to flop. It's been a long day."

"It has. Hey, what happened with you and the delay? Why were you on a later flight?"

Laurie sighed. "Gabe and I looked at another house outside of San Francisco. It took longer than we thought. We got caught in traffic, and I missed the flight. I was not a nice person to be around."

"Well, you're here now. That's all that matters. And what about the house? Do you like it?"

Gabe and Laurie had been talking about moving closer to

the city for several years. None of the previous leads on houses or property had suited them well enough to prompt them to uproot from the Napa Valley, where they both had lived all their lives.

"It's a fabulous house. The entryway is breathtaking—Italian marble with a fountain—and it has enough acreage for Gabe to build the studio of his dreams."

"Sounds gorgeous."

Laurie gave a shrug. "I suppose. It's just that I'm not too excited about the whole idea of moving. I've told you that before. This house has plenty of potential, so I'm trying to be open, but I'm still not convinced we should move. I can't believe our Realtor has been so patient with us. We have to be the pickiest clients she's ever had."

The elevator door opened, and we headed down the hall to our room. I hoped Laurie wasn't still in a "picky" mood when she saw the room because the decor definitely wasn't for those with more discriminating taste.

"So, what do you think?" I asked after Laurie had a moment to stand in the center of the room and absorb the full impact of the flower-power ambience.

"Audacious!" she exclaimed with a sparkle in her tone.

I laughed. "Now there's a descriptive word I haven't heard in a long time."

"I love it! I think they used this exact room to film one of the scenes in *Blue Hawaii.*"

When I didn't respond, she said, "You know, Elvis."

"Right! I thought the same thing."

Laurie looked at me with a patronizing grin. She knew I'd never seen an Elvis film in my life. "I have to take a picture." Laurie pulled several cameras from her shoulder bag.

"How many cameras did you bring?"

"Three. They're all different. This one is digital, the one with the yellow tape has black-and-white film, and the one with the big lens has color film and is the one I use the most."

"You're becoming serious about photography."

"They each serve a different purpose. You're welcome to borrow any of them, whenever you want. Now, stand over there by the wall, would you?"

"Me?"

"Yes, of course you. You don't mind, do you?"

"Only if you take it from the neck up."

Laurie laughed. "Wait. I have an idea." She pulled the red and white hibiscus-dotted bedspread off the bed. "If you wrap yourself in this and stand against the wall just right, you'll blend in. Your head will be the only thing showing."

Don't ask me why this seemed like a good idea or why I so willingly went along with it. Laurie could be persuasive when it came to stage direction. I complied as she wrapped little Emilee and me in the gaudy bedspread cocoon. She kept moving me, trying to match the hibiscus on the fabric with the hibiscus on the wallpaper. The purple orchid lei was distracting, so it came off.

"I can't believe I spent an entire day flying to Hawai'i only to spend my night allowing you to turn me into a human wall-flower."

"This is going to be hilarious." Laurie took a shade off one of the end table lamps and moved the lamp this way and that until she got the lighting the way she wanted. "Now don't move."

The thing about digital cameras is that you never know if the person is done with the shot or not because you don't hear a click.

"Just a second." Laurie stepped over to the doorway.

I thought she was turning on more lights. Instead, she opened the door and let the bellman in with her luggage.

"Hello?" I called out.

Like a mummy come back to life, I frantically twisted and turned my way out of the bedspread wrap. The floral prop puddled on the floor. I stepped away from it as if the wild thing had simply sprung from the bed on its own, and I was trying to get out of the way.

"No, that's fine," Laurie said. "You can leave the luggage right here by the door. Here you go. Thank you. Good night." She shooed off the bellman before he could step far enough into the room to see what was going on around the corner.

"Sorry about that," Laurie said to me. "Do you want to see the picture?"

I looked at the screen on her digital camera, and my long-time suspicion was confirmed. Laurie had a gift. A quirky gift, but a gift nonetheless. My head looked as if it were floating in a sea of garish hibiscus. Laurie said my head appeared to be tacked to the wall by the ends of my flippy hair.

I couldn't help but admire her natural, albeit peculiar, talent. "You are amazing. With you, a camera could be a deadly weapon, if you wanted to ruin your friends."

"Not ruin them. Capture them for one moment of life."

"You can erase it now."

Laurie gave me her best pout. "Do I have to? This is too fun, Hope. Please? I won't show it to anyone unless you say I can."

"Well, okay. You can keep it. E-mail me a copy. But don't turn it into screen savers or mouse pads or anything."

"I promise I won't."

An insightful woman would have seen all the signs after such an encounter and realized that Laurie was on the brink of something. I, on the other hand, was simply on the brink of exhaustion. It was almost one in the morning back in Connecticut.

Assuming pardon and grace would be extended to a cheeky pregnant woman, I nodded toward the disheveled bed next to the wall and said, "Do you mind if I take the bed by the window?"

Six

The pleasant, lulling sound of the endless ocean rocked me to sleep while Laurie took a bath and unpacked. Wrapping my arms around my middle, I lay still, waiting to see if Emilee might start her midnight butterfly dance. The boys did the same dance. As soon as I stopped moving, they would wake up and flutter around inside. Tonight, however, Emilee slept deeply, and so did I.

When I woke, it was still dark outside. The clock radio showed me three blurry numbers: 5:32. I closed my eyes and did the math. East Coast time was five hours ahead: 10:32. If I were at home, I would consider this sleeping in. I felt rested and energetic.

Laurie appeared to be sound asleep. In the stillness, I stretched out on my back with a hand on my tummy. Emilee greeted me with a tickling flutter, followed by a definite push of a hand or foot.

Good morning, little princess. Did you sleep as well as the runaway princess in the bed beside us?

I padded to the bathroom, changed into shorts and a T-shirt, and tiptoed back across the room in the silence of the predawn darkness. Slowly opening the sliding glass door, I ventured onto the lanai. Below me, the thundering ocean gleamed like obsidian in the artificial light cast on it from the hotel. I held on to the railing, bracing myself as the damp wind raced up my bare legs and puffed out my T-shirt. This was a completely different world from the one I'd watched in this same spot twelve hours earlier.

What a difference light makes.

I wanted the day to come. I wanted to see it come.

Standing straight, I felt like the only human on guard, like a sailor who was exploring the ends of the earth. I would stay right here, in my elevated crow's nest, scanning the horizon while the rest of the crew slept below deck. I would be the first one to spot the dawn.

I thought of my boys. My men. All four of them had been at school now for a few hours. Had they managed to find clean socks and pack their own lunches? My thoughts turned into prayers, which I whispered reverently like a simple morning song sent out across the waters.

As if a returning echo to my prayers, I heard a faint, melodic call sent out by a single bird in the darkness. A breath later, an echo came. This song was from a different bird with a different pitch, resonating a glad response. As I stood in a pocket of holy stillness, there rose on the softening winds a symphony of exultant twitters, chirps, and calls. The birds were welcoming the new day with me. Or perhaps it was I who was joining them in their morning worship.

I knew I had to go down to the water. I had to be there, front row, to see this day come.

"Laurie." I gently touched her shoulder. "I'm going to walk on the beach."

"What time is it?"

"Early. The sun hasn't come up yet."

"Then what are you doing up?"

"I'm not tired. You don't have to get up. I wanted to let you know where I was going."

Laurie pulled the covers back up to her chin. "Have a good time. And take your cell phone."

"Okay. Call me if you want anything. Oh, and happy birthday, Princess Laurie."

She smiled and went back to sleep.

It took only a few minutes to collect what I needed. I was down the elevator, through the lobby, past the pool, and onto the sand in what felt like one swift, unbroken motion.

The instant I stepped onto the beach I was shod with a custom-fit pair of sand booties for my bare feet. In front of me, at the water's edge, a wavy line as white as chalk traced the waves. I moved closer, wedged my feet into the wet, and waited for the cool salt water to push the sand up to my ankles.

I shivered and drew in deep breaths of the salty air. Twisting my feet deeper into the wet sand, I waited.

First light came from behind me.

"Mauka," I murmured. "From the mountains."

Then the sun rose, feeling like a warm hand on my shoulder, on my neck, on the top of my head. I fixed my gaze on the ocean and watched as rows of rising clouds lifted their gray nightshirts and shamelessly fluffed up their ruffled petticoats.

To the left of me, proud Diamond Head, the prow of this anchored isle, stretched bodice-first into the sea. The sunlight rolled across the sides of the darkened knoll, transforming the deep browns into a tapestry of greens and grays and bronze.

A young couple strolled by, hand in hand, with their backs to Diamond Head. A hunched man wearing a sweatshirt and faded shorts methodically passed a metal detector over the sand. A young woman jogged toward me, chattering on her cell phone.

You're missing it! I wanted to call out to all of them. *Look, it's a new day!*

"*Pohuehue*," said a warm voice behind me.

I hadn't heard the old woman approach. She stood only a few feet away, with her face to the ocean and hands behind her back. She wore a simple mu'umu'u and a bright wreath of flowers around her head. The morning light illuminated her white hair with a diaphanous glow.

"You see it, don't you?" she said to me.

I nodded hesitantly, not sure what I saw or who was asking me.

Taking slow, even steps, she came and stood beside me. "This is our word for such a morning: *pohuehue.*"

"Is that Hawaiian for 'beautiful'?" I asked.

"No." She shook her radiant head. "It is Hawaiian for 'beach morning glory.' There is no equal word in English."

"Po-hue-hue," I repeated under my breath.

"You see it, don't you?"

"Yes." I felt at ease with this woman.

She smiled.

We stood together, silently watching.

In a blink, the sun had risen to just the right angle so that spears of radiant light pierced the foaming curl of the morning waves, transforming the sea into a silver-laced field of turquoise blue.

Then, just as the birds had sung before the first light, the woman beside me drew in a deep breath and projected her rich, warbling voice across the waters. "*He Akua hemolele.*" Her song was as deep as the ocean itself. "*He Akua hemolele. Ke Akua no kakou.*"

I didn't know what image I'd imprinted on my mind of what I thought it would be like to finally stroll the beach at Waikiki after twenty years of anticipating it, but it was nothing like this. I had never imagined an encounter with a Hawaiian woman who would fill the morning air with such delightful reverence. I never dreamed this world held such spectacular "beach morning glory." I felt alive with the sensations that now enfolded me. God seemed so close. The calm breeze felt like His breath on my neck.

I wanted to dance. I know that sounds silly, but the song of this surprising old woman was going inside me, making me want to stretch my arms to the heavens and give movement to all my heightened senses.

But sensibility restrained me.

What would the other early-morning tourists here on the beach think of me? I'd look like an unbalanced woman, twirling around with a big bubble in my middle.

So I stood still and didn't move. The joy slowly dissipated from my spirit. The desire to dance fell away. The song of my morning companion ended.

"That was beautiful," I said, barely above a whisper.

"*Mahalo.*" She smiled at me.

"I wish I understood Hawaiian so I'd know what you just sang."

"It is not a great mystery. I was singing words that come from the Bible."

"What part?"

"Psalms. One hundred and four."

With a few more buttery words in Hawaiian, the woman leaned close to me and breathed out the word, "Aloha." Then she turned and continued her trek down the beach.

I closed my eyes and opened them again. I wasn't dreaming. This strange and wonderful morning really was happening.

My cell phone rang in my shorts pocket, and I knew I was still in the real world. It was Laurie.

"Look up," she said.

I looked at the sky over the ocean.

"No, behind you. Look up at the hotel," she said laughing.

The beach was lined with one tall hotel after another. For Laurie to stand on our lanai and spot me on the nearly deserted beach was one thing. For me to look up and distinguish which lanai was attached to our hotel room was another thing altogether.

But that Laurie! She had hung the red floral bedspread over the railing and was waving it at me like a banner of freedom.

"Laurie, you better not drop that bedspread!"

"I have a good grip on it. What do you think? Does it look better from a distance?"

"Gorgeous. Or what was your word? Ostentatious!"

"No, my word was *audacious*. But *ostentatious* works, too. So who was that you were talking to?"

"I don't know. I honestly thought she was an angel at first. Not that I've ever seen an angel. But, Laurie, it was bizarre in a wonderful way. She appeared out of nowhere and was all lit up, and she sang over the ocean." I realized I was using my free arm to gesture as if Laurie could see me clearly from her perch.

"Hope, look behind you."

I turned to see several early-morning strollers stopped in their tracks watching, as I appeared to be talking to the hotel, using big arm motions and saying I had seen an angel.

"It's my roommate." I held out my cell phone and nodded toward the lanai. "Do you see the one with the bright red bedspread?"

That Laurie! She had pulled in all the colors. I could hear her laughing over the phone, tucked away in the privacy of our hotel room.

"I can't believe you did that!" I walked quickly toward the hotel, masking my laughter. "Just because it's your birthday, don't think you can get away with all kinds of Waikiki wackiness. I was your wallflower last night, but I'm not posing for you anymore."

"Waikiki wackiness?" Laurie repeated. "Hey, I'm not the one strolling around before dawn looking for angels."

"I wasn't looking for angels. She found me. You saw her. She was a real person. I had a very spiritual moment, so don't ruin it for me."

"Okay, I won't. Hey, do you want to bring some breakfast back up with you? Or should I order room service?"

"I'll bring something. What's your request, Miss Birthday Princess?"

"Coffee. Tall, dark, and caffeinated."

"Anything else?"

"Yes, something full of sugar and butter and white flour. Doesn't matter what shape it takes. Throw in some chocolate, and I'd say my four basic vacation food groups will be covered."

"Not dieting this week?"

"No, I'm going to eat whatever I want and not regret a single bite. Go ahead, surprise me with something decadent."

Laurie had no complaints about the coffee and the chocolate-filled croissant I picked up for her at the espresso cart in the lobby. I also brought an assortment of brochures from the concierge, which we spread out on my tidy bed to discuss our options for the week after we enjoyed our breakfast on the lanai.

"Didn't you get yourself a coffee?" Laurie watched me take a sip of my bottled water.

"No, I packed some loose tea, but I only want water right now."

"Of course you brought loose tea with you. Any chance you brought some Ladybug tea?"

"As a matter of fact, I did."

I went into the room where I pulled two small wrapped gifts from my nearly emptied suitcase. "Happy birthday," I said, handing the presents to Laurie.

"Hey, I thought we agreed we weren't going to give each other presents. This trip is our present to each other, remember? That's what you said."

"I know. It's just some Ladybug tea and another little something. Go ahead, open them."

Laurie peeled back the wrapping on a small framed photo of the two of us that was taken our freshman year of college.

"Look at us! We were so young! Look at our hair! Where did you find this?"

"In a box. I came across it a few months ago and had a copy made. I have a duplicate on my dresser at home."

"I love it. Thanks, Hope. What a treasure. Thanks for the tea. I'm almost out. I haven't asked you how things have been at work. What's been happening at the Ladybug Tea and Cakes?"

"It's been slow, but it always is in January."

"I know you know this, but I love bragging about you and how you and your neighbor started with nothing more than a loan from the bank and a lot of renovations provided by your husband."

"We paid off the loan last month. Did I tell you that?"

"Hope, that's incredible. Do you know how many small businesses go under in the first five years?"

"No, and don't tell me. Our little teahouse will start its fifth year in May, so we're not out of the disaster statistics yet."

"But you're doing something you love, you're successful at it, and you're still able to be home when you want. You're living a dream, Hope. I wish I could find something like that to do. I feel so…so…"

I looked over at Laurie, and right behind her a brilliant rainbow had appeared. It seemed to form a perfect arch over her head like a tiara. Reaching for her camera strung over the back of her chair I said, "Laurie, whatever you do, don't move."

Seven

What is it? A bug? A spider? It's not one of those gecko lizards, is it?" Laurie had never done well with creepy, crawling creatures.

"It's a rainbow," I said. "You have a rainbow coming out of your eyebrow, and I want to capture it. Hold still."

"Coming out of my eyebrow? Hope, don't line up the shot so that it looks freaky."

"What? You don't want to look like you're growing strange, multicolor appendages out of your forehead?"

"Let me think…No!" She grabbed for the camera and turned to face the rainbow. "Oh, that is gorgeous!"

"I told you."

"It's gorgeous because it's right there, hanging in the sky, all by itself, where it's supposed to be. If it were shooting out of my eyebrow, it would no longer look gorgeous."

A ringing in my pocket interrupted our banter. I pulled out

my cell phone and was surprised to see Darren's name appear on my caller screen.

"Hi, is everything okay?"

"We're fine," he said. "What about you?"

"Great! Laurie and I are having breakfast on the lanai, and one of us—" I gave Laurie a little smirk—"is trying to take pictures of a rainbow."

"So, you got there okay?" Darren sounded edgy.

"Yes. We both got here with only a few problems, but everything is fine."

"I hadn't heard from you, so I didn't know if everything was okay."

"Darren, I'm sorry. I should have called when I arrived last night. I figured it would be so late at home that you would be in bed."

"I probably was still up," he said quietly. "I'm glad everything is going well."

"Yes. It's beautiful here."

"Okay. Well, the boys are fine, and I'm fine. We're out of dish soap. Other than that, everything is fine."

My big, tough husband sounded like a lost puppy. Who would have guessed it? I wondered if I might be appreciated more when I got home. Not a bad thing, with a baby on the way.

"I love you," I told him.

"I love you, too. Have a good time."

"We will. Bye."

"Everything okay?" Laurie asked.

"They're out of dish soap."

"Oh." She gave a knowing nod. "That happens sometimes."

"You better call Gabe before he calls here next."

"I already did. Called at the airport as soon as the plane landed. Rule number one: Always call home the minute the plane lands."

"Really. And what's rule number two?"

"Never laugh about anything when they call. Try to sound a little tired, a little sad."

"Okay."

"Rule number three is always: Tell them you miss them and that you love them. You have to say the part about missing them first before they believe you about the loving them."

"Got it. So, how did you get so wise in matters of the home?"

Laurie leaned back in her chair and gazed toward the ocean with a regal air. "It must be the gift of old age. You'll find out soon enough, my dear."

Her stately profile was perfectly lined up so that the lingering rainbow now appeared to come right out of her nose. I grabbed the camera and took the shot.

Rule number one: Never ask Laurie if you can take her picture. Just take it.

She turned to check on the rainbow and then glared at me. "You didn't make it look like that rainbow was coming out of my eyebrow, did you?"

"No," I answered. "It wasn't coming out of your eyebrow."

That was when I realized why I enjoyed Laurie so much. I was raised with two younger brothers. Or perhaps I should say I helped raise two younger brothers. Now I was raising three boys. Growing up, my dearest, secret wish had been to have a sister. A twin, preferably.

When Laurie and I felt close enough as college roomies to have yelling matches over who was leaving junk on whose side of the room, I realized my wish had come true. Laurie was the closest thing to a real sister I would ever know. I adored her.

"What do you want to do today?" I asked the birthday girl.

She drew in a deep breath. "I think I want to show you something. Wait here."

I gazed at the ocean while she went into the bedroom. I kept thinking about the rainbow displacement shot and reveled in the delicious anticipation of hearing Laurie squeak when I got the photos developed. I determined I would borrow her camera often in the next few days. That way I'd finish off a roll and suggest we take it to a one-hour photo lab.

I could feel the side of my left leg heating up. Even though the day was still young, the sun's intensity made me nervous about getting branded with a strange sunburn splotch on my thigh.

"Laurie, could you grab my sunscreen while you're in there?"

She returned with the lotion and a brown leather portfolio. "This is what I want to show you. Please don't put on the lotion yet; it might leave marks on these if it's still on your fingers."

I turned so the sun wasn't hitting my leg directly and opened the portfolio. Inside was a stack of enlarged photographs. The first one was in black and white and focused on a fascinating pair of weathered hands tearing off a piece of bread. I couldn't take my eyes off the photo.

"That's Gabe's grandmother. I took it three summers ago. Don't say anything yet. Just take a look."

I noted that Laurie had identified the picture as being Gabe's grandmother. She didn't say it was his grandmother's hands, but rather it was his grandmother. Going through the pictures one by one, she continued to label each person with the shot, even though the photo was of only part of that person. The part represented the whole.

My favorite was the one of Gabe with their black Labrador when Trooper was a puppy. The focus was on Gabe's chin, neck, and part of his shoulder. His head was tilted all the way back, his mouth open in full laughter, and the puppy's pink tongue was just about to go in for another tickle-lick of Gabe's neck.

"Laurie, these are absolutely amazing. Incredible! You told me you were taking lots of pictures lately, but I thought you meant a bunch of snapshots for a scrapbook or something. You're very good at capturing the essence of the person or the moment. I'm blown away at how magnificent these are."

"Do you really think so, Hope?" Her gaze was critical. A valley had formed between her eyebrows. "You're not just saying that."

"No! Of course not."

She bit her thumbnail. "I knew you would be honest with me. Tell me you're being honest with me."

"Of course I'm being honest. You know that I am. These are exceptionally wonderful photos, and you should do something with them."

"Like what?"

"I don't know. What does Gabe think?"

Laurie shook her head. The deep crevice remained between her stormy brows.

"What? He doesn't like them?"

"He hasn't seen them."

"Why not?"

Laurie closed up the portfolio, took it away from me, and went into the room.

I followed her. "Why haven't you shown these to Gabe?"

"I don't think I could bear it if he said anything negative about them. I show him the other family shots I take. But I always pull out the special few. I've been saving them."

"You've been hiding them," I corrected her.

I could tell Laurie didn't like what I said, but she took it from me like a champ. "Okay, hiding them. I've been hiding the pictures and saving them for just the right moment to show Gabe. I decided to bring them and show you first. I thought you could coach me on how to work up the courage to show Gabe."

"Why are you so afraid of his criticism? Maybe I don't understand, but it's art, right? You've told me before that art is subjective. If someone doesn't like it, that's his preference."

"I know, but Gabe is…well, you know, he's the master painter. The sought-after artist. He's the creative one in our family. I just make life happen for everyone else. But now I have these photos, and they're burning a hole in my heart."

I studied Laurie's expression. "You have more, don't you? More than just the dozen you brought to show me."

Her mouth twitched slightly.

"How many photos do you have?"

"Two hundred and fifty-nine."

"Laurie!"

"What?"

I went across the room and sat next to her on the edge of her unmade bed. How could I nudge her forward on this? I didn't understand her timidity.

"Laurie, you realize, don't you, that what you have here is not a hobby. This is a gift. A calling. I don't understand why you haven't pursued getting them displayed or at least framed."

"I really love these pictures, Hope."

"I can tell."

"As long as I keep them tucked away like my own little treasure, then no one can reject them or criticize them. I've seen what Gabe has gone through over the years. Everybody has an opinion. Every dealer has a price. I've watched him struggle with his work becoming less of an art and more of a commodity. I'm not sure I could bear that kind of pressure."

"Laurie, you're projecting way, way out there. It doesn't have to be overly commercial for you."

"But my name…"

"What about your name?"

"Giordani. Don't you think it would catapult me into a big arena, if I showed up with some art with the Giordani name on it?"

"Don't sign them with Giordani. Sign them 'photos by Laurie' or use your given name—Laurinda Sue. You don't have to ride in Gabe's wake. Start your own tsunami."

She didn't look convinced.

"Okay, not a tsunami. Your own little ripple, then. The point is, you know in your gut that you have to do something with this gift. Otherwise, it wouldn't be burning a hole in you, and you wouldn't have brought them here to show me."

"You're right, Hope."

"It's like you're carrying around this 259-pound baby that you want to protect from the big, bad world. And you know what? You just have to give birth and trust God for what's going to happen after that."

"I wasn't going to show them to you until later in the week," Laurie said with a sniff.

"I'm glad you brought them out when you did. I love them. You have created amazing works of art. Each one evokes deep emotion. You know what your pictures do? They invite people to worship by focusing on intricate details of God's creation. You've been entrusted with this gift, Laurie.

You must be a good steward and do something with it."

She nodded.

I could tell I was going into challenge overload. I had the tendency to do that after living so long with a coach. Women need a lot less overt pushing than men, but I often forgot that.

"I'm done." I gave her arm a squeeze. "Let's go do something fun. We have some birthday celebrating to do." I reached for one of the brochures. "Outrigger canoeing, anyone?"

Eight

*L*aurie opted for the catamaran instead of the outrigger canoe. We called the concierge and signed up for a late morning sail, which was departing in half an hour.

"I'll be quick." Laurie disappeared into the bathroom. I had a flashback to college days when Laurie would change outfits a minimum of three times a day. Neither of us had a lot of clothes to select from back then, but it always took her twice as long to get ready for class.

I put on my swimsuit with a glance in the mirror that hung above the wicker dresser. The reflection woman looking back didn't give me the slightest peep of sass. Apparently these Hawaiian hotel mirrors have much better manners than the mirrors they sell in Connecticut.

My cover-up was one of Darren's long-sleeved, white cotton shirts, which I'd confiscated at the last minute. I put on my maternity shorts and my all-terrain sandals. Reaching for my bottle of suntan lotion and my sunglasses, I was ready to hit the beach. Hobo-style.

Laurie emerged in a classy one-piece black swimsuit with a long, sheer wraparound skirt in black with gold swirls. All she needed was to put her lei around her neck, and she would look like she was on her way to a photo shoot for the cover of a resort apparel catalog.

Slipping her small feet into a pair of black strappy sandals she said, "Remind me to buy a pair of flip-flops at the gift shop. These are the only sandals I brought, and they aren't very practical for walking in the sand."

"You want practical? How about these four-wheel drive Hummers here?" I held out a foot, modeling my industrial-strength leather sandals. "These are indestructible. Darren says they were designed by some organic Oregonian and come with a fifty-two-year warranty."

"A fifty-two-year warranty? Really?"

"No, not really. That's my husband's idea of a joke. They don't come with a warranty of any kind. All I know is that they're supposed to keep my posture in proper alignment. They're nice and practical for a frump-mama, but not at all dainty or cute."

"Hey, you are nowhere close to being a frump-mama! Seriously, Hope, you look great. I've never seen your skin so radiant. All you need is a pedicure and some glimmery polish on those toenails, and you'll feel like a new woman."

"Is that your charm school secret?" I asked, looking at her pampered feet.

"It couldn't hurt. When was the last time you had a pedicure?"

I grinned at Laurie, as she gathered up her beach bag and turned to look at me, waiting for an answer.

"Never."

"Seriously? You've never had a pedicure?"

"No."

"You've never gone to a salon of any sort and had your feet taken care of?"

"No."

"That settles it; I know what I'm getting you for your birthday."

"We aren't giving each other gifts, remember?"

"Oh, right, but you already broke that rule, remember?"

I grinned. "How about if we both get pedicures?"

"Fine."

We rode the elevator to the lobby in a funny little conversation gap. It was as if we'd entered a dome of silence. I was contemplating what it would have been like if Laurie and I had come to Hawai'i when we were twenty. Before Gabriel, before Darren, before our children, and before all of the other crazy, life-defining stuff.

I was glad we were here now instead of during the manic young-adult years. Even with the aqua swimsuit under my husband's wrinkled shirt, my all-terrain sandals, and my never-been-manicured toes, I was beginning to feel comfortable inside my own skin. It was a feeling I liked.

The hotel pool area was crowded. We wove our way down to the beach activities booth on the sand and checked in for our sail. A large catamaran awaited us, only a few yards away.

"You're the ones," the activities assistant said.

"Are we late?" I asked.

"No, I meant you're the ones who just signed up, right?"

"Right."

"It's good that you called because only four other people were signed up, and the guys won't take out the cat unless they have at least six paying passengers. So we're glad you signed up."

"How many passengers do they usually take out?"

"They can hold up to thirty-eight, but we usually keep it to twenty-five or so."

"Sounds like we're going to have the sailboat to ourselves," I said.

"Catamaran," the activities assistant corrected me with an edge to her voice. "There is a difference."

We soon discovered some of those differences, as Laurie and I boarded the gleaming white craft that motored out to sea, floating on the two buoyant hulls. The boat's overall surface was flat with a wide, woven mesh at the front, which was occupied by two teenage girls wearing itsy-bitsy, teeny-weeny bikinis. The two other passengers were an elderly Asian couple who had made themselves comfortable on the padded bench seats inside the belly of the catamaran.

Laurie and I sat outside, toward the back, getting our bearings and watching the crew, which consisted of two buff young men and one skinny young woman wearing a two-piece bathing suit in lifeguard red and a bandana around her neck. I'm not sure what her fashion statement was, but it seemed to work for her.

As soon as we were far enough out on the water, the crew ran up the colorful sail, and the boat skimmed along. I held on and felt the wind pulling my hair in every direction. Laurie looked exhilarated. She always did have a need for speed.

"Any chance you want to go up there to the front?" She nodded toward the mesh area where the girls were ducking their heads and squealing each time a wave came up and splashed them.

"Go ahead, if you want. I think I'd better stay right here until we slow down a little." I didn't trust my equilibrium to get me all the way to the front of the catamaran without falling into the water.

The boat tacked in another direction. The two guys adjusted the sail, and our speed slowed to a gentle bobbing along on the big blue sea rather than trying to leave skid marks on the water.

Waikiki's shoreline had diminished behind us, looking like a puppet stage designed by an imaginative child. The buildings stood like rows of colorful LEGOs, left midway through their construction by a youthful creator who had outgrown the project before it was completed.

All around us, before us, above us, below us, the world was blue.

"Something to drink?" one of the guys on the crew asked us.

"Sure," I responded.

"We have an ice chest of beverages in the galley, and we set out some *puu puus.*"

"Some what?" Laurie asked.

"Snacks. If you know what you want, I'll bring it to you."

"That's okay. We can go and get something," Laurie said.

Now that the catamaran had slowed down, I was curious to see the insides of the craft. The older couple nodded as we entered the spacious cabin. To steady myself, I sat beside the woman.

"This is nice in here," I said. "Cool and quiet."

The woman nodded.

I reached for a potato chip and munched away.

"Do you want some water, Hope, or something else?"

"Water sounds good."

Laurie brought me a cold bottle. We sat a moment, trying to politely nibble the chips and skim the surface of the creamy dip with baby carrots but not make a mess. We couldn't tell if we were interrupting this couple, or if they were just being quiet. Down in the more stable hull, the wind wasn't blowing. The sun wasn't shining. The blue was gone.

"This doesn't feels like sailing," I whispered to Laurie. "Let's go back up where the wind is blowing."

Nodding to the sedate couple, Laurie and I returned topside, slowly making our way to the front. If we were going to be on the ocean, I wanted to feel like we were out where the action was happening. I couldn't imagine how packed this vessel would be with twenty-five or more passengers.

Laurie had planted herself on the mesh netting, and I was making my way toward her with my wobbly legs, when one of the teen girls beside us let out a shriek. "Shark!"

I grabbed the railing and held on, trying to stay out of the way while one of the crew guys hopped across the mesh to look into the water. He laughed. "It's a school of dolphins."

Laurie helped me sit beside her, and we leaned over to see the putty-colored creatures gliding effortlessly alongside the catamaran.

"They're so graceful," Laurie said. "It's like they're trying to race us."

"Look how the light makes them shine," I said. "The water is so clear. I just want to reach over and touch one of them."

For a long stretch, the dolphins kept in perfect formation, escorting us as we sailed along.

"What kind are they?" Laurie asked the young woman on the crew who had joined us to watch.

"Spinner," the young woman said. "We haven't seen any out here for a while. I've missed them."

One of the guys on the crew started to tease her. "I'm sure they missed you, little haole girl."

"Hey, who you calling a haole girl?"

"You, haole girl," he said.

She gave the guy a friendly shove. "You watch it, *da' kine* boy, or you'll go in for a swim with the dolphins."

They joked back and forth while the dolphins slowed their pace and fell away from us. I scanned the water for any sign of the friendly creatures, but as quickly as they had appeared, they disappeared.

"See what you did?" the clever girl with the bandana around her neck said to the guy. "You scared 'em away."

"Not me. You scared 'em, haole girl." The guy had such a great smile and easygoing manner that it seemed he was enjoying the teasing as much as the girl was.

"May I ask you a question?" I said. "What does *how-lee* mean?"

"No breath," the island boy said.

"No breath?" I repeated.

The girl turned toward me. "It's what the Hawaiians call someone who is just visiting the islands. Someone who isn't a local. It's not a very polite term." She gave the guy another punch in the arm.

"Auwe!" He cried in mock pain, rubbing his arm.

"You big baby."

"Hey!" the other crewmate called from the back of the catamaran, breaking up the little flirt-fest. "Somebody check on the line on the port. It looks like it's tangled."

"You check it." The guy gave a chin-up nod to the girl.

"Fine. I'll show you how it's done."

He kept grinning as she made her way across the mesh

with ease. It was a rather entertaining pleasure to watch these two interact. It made me think of Darren and the way he had perfected the art of teasing when we first met. I was the short-stop for our church summer league softball team, and Darren was on second base. He says the night he watched me slide into home and scrape up my leg was the night he knew I was the one for him. I couldn't imagine sliding anywhere or scraping any part of me on purpose now. I wondered if Darren missed the old Hope.

For the remainder of our catamaran sail, Laurie and I stayed in the front, even though we got splashed and our hair was tousled like crazy while the sail billowed with the steady trade wind and took us coasting in to shore.

"I like your hair like that," Laurie said, as the catamaran slowly motored back into its watery parking spot near the beach.

"You're kidding, right?"

"No, it's darling. You should see it."

I fluffed up the sides and tugged at the wayward strands in the back. "You like it?"

"I really do. Seriously."

"I call it 'swims with dolphins.'"

"Well, it's working for you, girl." Laurie hopped up off the mesh. "I'll get our beach bags."

I rolled to the side, trying to find a useable center of gravity. First to the left...nothing to hold on to. I rolled to the right. And rolled some more, until I was in the center of the mesh, with canvas and gravity playing a joke on me. I was stuck. The other four tourists were off the catamaran and saying their thank-yous to the crew.

"Laurie," I called out, calmly at first. She didn't hear me inside the cabin. "Laurie!" She still didn't hear.

I tried to reach for one of the ropes hanging from the mast pole, thinking I could use it to pull myself up.

"Whoa, not that one," the island boy said, coming toward me with that huge white smile of his at full sail. "You need a hand?"

"Yes," I said with as much dignity as I could muster. "As a matter of fact, I *could* use a hand. Thank you."

The brawny island boy didn't hold out a hand for me. Oh, no, he came around behind me, looped his thick arms under my perspiring armpits and hoisted me up, using his knee to support my lower back. I had no choice but to depend on his broad chest to steady my disoriented sense of balance.

Click.

Click, click, click, click.

That Laurie! She couldn't manage to come back and offer assistance in my time of need, but she was right on the spot when it came to a photo op.

Lowering the camera, she grinned at me. "Swims with dolphins, huh?"

Nine

After the invigorating voyage and a good laugh strolling through the sand, Laurie and I decided to plant our still-loopy selves into a couple of anchored lounge chairs. A poolside waitress wearing itty-bitty shorts and a tank top came over. I asked what kind of tropical drinks they had without alcohol.

"But with an umbrella," Laurie added.

"Right, with an umbrella. That's the most important ingredient."

The waitress pulled a small laminated menu from the back pocket of her shorts and handed it to me.

"This first one with the coconut and pineapple juice sounds good," I said. "I'll have one of those."

"Make it two," Laurie said.

As the young woman strolled off, Laurie leaned over. "Did you see how she made that menu appear out of thin air? How did she do that? She didn't have enough room in her tiny back pocket to hold that card."

"No kidding."

"What do you think? Sleight of hand? Smoke and mirrors?"

"I don't know," I said. "But I don't think I ever managed to fit into a pair of shorts that small. Not even in second grade."

"Oh, I beg to differ. What about those fluorescent green ones you used to wear to go jogging? Remember? The nylon ones with the matching terry cloth headband?"

"Oh, yeah. I forgot about those."

"How could you forget?"

"Be kind, Laurie. It was the eighties."

"Hey, I know. I was there, too, remember?"

"What I remember is the time we sat up all night trying to braid those beads into your hair. The next day in chemistry one of the rows came undone, and you dropped beads every time you moved your head."

Laurie's laugh switched to a groan. "Oh, that was such a mess. I couldn't figure out which string had come undone, and when I tried to take all of them out, I lost so much hair. Remember how all those little strands were twisted around the beads? I can't believe I did that. What was I thinking?"

"You were thinking you were cool because you were."

"We were both cool." Laurie looked at me over the top rim of her glasses. "We were both cool then, and we are both very cool now."

"The coolest," I agreed.

"Except for when we wore those spandex leggings with the big hot-pink T-shirts." Laurie made a face. "There *is* no excuse for that."

With ideal timing, the waitress returned carrying our tropical drinks, just when we needed to toast something important.

"To friendship that spans the decades." Laurie raised her umbrella-accented tropical drink.

"And to friendship that spans further than our current hip measurements."

We merrily tapped the rims of our plastic cups and took our first sip. The beverage tasted like a thick, sweet smoothie with bits of pineapple pulp that clogged the straw. I liked it.

Laurie plucked her paper umbrella from her cup and tucked it behind her right ear. "So, where are you supposed to wear these to show that you're taken?"

I held my tiny umbrella on the pinnacle of my blue, mountain belly. "Right here should work pretty good for me."

"Oh yes, like it worked so swimmingly for you back there on the sailboat."

"Catamaran," I corrected her with an edge in my voice like the activities director who checked us in for the sail had used. "There *is* a difference."

We laughed, and I felt a familiar sensation returning.

"I'll be right back." It was easy to roll out of the lounge chair and slip my feet into my wide sandals.

"I admire what you're doing, Hope."

"What, going to the bathroom every twenty minutes?"

"No. I think you're amazing for being pregnant and still doing all this. Coming to Hawai'i, I mean. I thought you might change your mind about the trip. I would have understood if you had, but you didn't back out, and I'm glad."

"I'm glad, too."

"I mean it, Hope. You are the bright, sheltering umbrella in the fruity slush of my life."

I gave her an appreciative grin over my shoulder and took the shortest route to the lobby rest room. When I returned, Laurie was eating a sandwich.

"Do you want a bite of this? It's really good."

"What did you order?"

"It's mahimahi with mango salsa in a veggie wrap."

"And what is mahimahi?"

"Fish. White fish."

"Is it cooked?"

"Of course it's cooked."

"I'm not sure Emilee would appreciate my trying sushi for the first time while she's still onboard."

"This is definitely cooked, and it's really mild. Here, have a bite."

After the first tiny bite, I was hooked. "That is so good."

"I know. Here, have the other half."

"You sure?"

"Yep. That way we'll have room for dessert."

Laurie looked past me and made a sweeping gesture. "It's really beautiful here, isn't it? Incredibly beautiful."

"Yes, it is."

"I didn't think it would be like the postcards, but it is. I love those trees. Plumeria, aren't they? They have such a great shape with their long, slender branches. And this sky is so blue. We rarely see it this blue at home."

"Same with us."

"We're really in Hawai'i, aren't we, Hope? We finally made it over here."

"Yes, we are in Hawai'i. Finally. And it is beautiful here. It's amazing what you start to notice as soon as you get a little pineapple in your system."

"Pineapple, nothing. It's this mango salsa."

"Right, the mango salsa."

"I have to take some pictures." Laurie finished her half of the fish sandwich and reached for her camera. Handing me my little umbrella she said, "Here, pop this behind one of your ears." Laurie always was big on props.

Since I was eager for her to use up that roll of film, I entered in willingly. "Which ear?"

"Either one. Doesn't matter."

I posed for her. "This will give us something to laugh about when we're sixty, right? I mean, if I could go jogging in public wearing skimpy lime green shorts at twenty and laugh about it when I'm forty, then I can pose in a maternity bathing suit at forty, and we can laugh about it when we're sixty."

"We won't laugh," Laurie said. "We'll say, 'Hey, we looked pretty good back then. Better than we do now!'"

"Do you honestly think we'll say that?"

Laurie put down the camera. "Yes, I do. We'll wonder why we were so self-conscious about our bodies when they were being so nice to us."

I was twisting the paper umbrella between my fingers, contemplating Laurie's comment, when she snapped the first picture.

"Hey, I wasn't ready."

She snapped another one. "Just pretend I'm not here. Think of how you and I are entering the era of being comfortable. This is the time in our lives when we should focus on contentment rather than appearance."

"Is that supposed to make me smile for the camera?"

Laurie kept talking with the camera in front of her face. "Gabe's mom says the first twenty years are all about charm. From twenty to forty, it's about beauty. Forty to sixty is the contentment season, and then sixty to eighty are the dignity years."

"That's profound."

"Yes, it is. More of my over-forty sage insights. Now put the umbrella behind your ear and give me your best Honolulu-mama grin."

From the profound to the fruity. I went for the left ear. "You know, I think you had a pair of earrings about this size our freshman year."

"Careful," Laurie said.

"They were bright yellow, weren't they?"

"How can you remember that?" She lowered the camera. "They were bright yellow with black stripes. All bees in Santa Barbara thought I was their mother."

I laughed, and she snapped another shot. Then a sound I'd been hoping for came to my ears. Laurie had hit the end of the roll, and the camera was automatically rewinding the film.

"We could see if the hotel has a one-hour developing service."

"No, that's okay, Hope. I prefer the service I use at home. I'll send you copies."

I knew then that my mission would be to snag that roll of film when Laurie wasn't looking and find a way to have it developed here.

Laurie put away her camera while I ambled over to the pool to wet my feet. I stepped into the shallow end and went down the steps until the cool water was up to my knees.

My legs were still white. Winter wonderland white. The clear pool water seemed only to emphasize that disturbing fact.

Laurie joined me, sitting on the edge of the pool and dangling her legs in the water. "I think the tops of my feet got sunburned," she said. "I always forget to put sunscreen on my feet. You look like you got some color on your face."

"Really?" I instinctively touched my cheeks. "It's probably my normal mama-glow instead of sun-glow. I seem to have no difficulty showing a little color in my face lately. It's these white legs I was hoping to bronze up."

Laurie's legs already were warming up with a deep glow the

color of Darjeeling tea with milk. The only warm tones that showed up in my skin were brown spotty freckles on my arms and legs.

"I have an idea," Laurie said. "Let's pop into the gift shop and buy some instant tan in a can for your legs."

"You just want to see that guy we embarrassed at the counter last night."

"Correction." Laurie scooped up a handful of pool water and let it fall over her knees. "The guy *you* embarrassed trying to purchase every home pregnancy test on the island."

"I don't think I can go back in there if he's working this afternoon. Poor kid."

"Then I'll go in," Laurie said. "I'll buy the tanner for you. Before you go home, your skin will be a gorgeous shade of happy cocoa beans. Everyone who comes into the Ladybug Tea and Cakes next week will say, 'My, my, don't you look tan! Where have you been?' And you can brag your little heart out and say—"

"Yeah, I'll say I went to Hawai'i, and my friend bought me a can of brown spray paint."

"It's not brown spray paint, Hope. It's foam. Or gel. Or lotion, or something."

"See? You don't even know because you've never used it."

"So? There's nothing wrong with a little enhancement of our natural beauty. It's mandatory if we're going to experience contentment in this next season of life."

"First you promise me a pedicure for my uncultured feet

and now cocoa-bean legs. How could I possibly turn down such an offer?"

"You can't. So don't fight it."

I wasn't going to fight it. If Laurie left to go to the gift shop, I could grab the roll of film. But she didn't go right then. Instead, she ordered more tropical beverages, and we started a little collection of paper umbrellas beside our lounge chairs at the pool.

Laurie's theory about the forty-to-sixty season seemed to be working. We were both quite content.

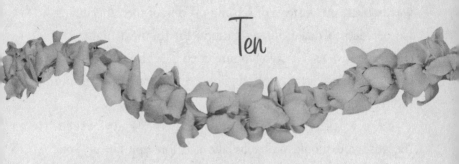

Ten

When I look back on the decision to use the artificial tanner, I remind myself that even though Laurie initially had the idea, I did give my full consent.

An older woman was running the register by the time we entered the gift shop in the late afternoon. No blushing young man appeared on the premises. That was a big disappointment to Laurie.

Of the two types of skin-bronzing formula available, Laurie recommended the smaller, more expensive one. Budget-minded me went for the larger, less expensive one, even though Laurie offered to pay for it. I told her she could treat me later to an ice cream cone or something. I felt funny having her buy an item that came from the "personal needs" section.

With the instant suntan in hand, Laurie and I stopped by the concierge desk to sign up for a luau that evening. To our dismay, the luau we had agreed offered everything we wanted was booked up. Instead of settling on one of the other luaus, we decided to make our reservation for the next night. The concierge gave us a list of recommended beachfront restaurants within walking distance of our hotel, and we returned to our room to get ready for dinner.

"Are you thinking of taking a shower?" Laurie asked. "Because you should probably take it before you tan up your legs so you don't wash it off too soon."

"Good idea."

I showered and thoroughly patted my legs dry before applying the heavily-scented lotion. It came out of the can in foam, and the little bubbles tingled as I smoothed them over my skin. I made sure to rub the color all the way up my legs so I wouldn't have an artificial tan line to go along with my artificial tan. I even covered my feet and toes.

Then, because it seemed silly to have cocoa-brown legs while the rest of me remained white, I went for further coverage. Arms first. Then shoulders and neck. I guessed that any part of me that could be seen in a bathing suit should be the same color. I stretched my arms to reach the back of my shoulders and my upper back.

My face was the final territory to conquer. I applied the foamy lotion generously, as the slightly metallic fragrance filled the small, fogged-up bathroom. Task completed, I wiped my hands on the white hand towel, and a burnt orange smear appeared. Sticking the towel under cold water, I was relieved to see that the mark diminished. The hotel certainly must bleach all their towels, so it wouldn't be a problem to lift out the final tinge. Nonetheless, I understood how my boys must feel when I lecture them about doing a better job with the soap and water before they dry their hands on the towel.

Laurie tapped on the bathroom door. "How's it going?"

"Good. I'm finished, if you're ready to get in here." I slipped into my robe and opened the door.

Laurie looked me over. "How long is it supposed to take?"

"Do you mean I'm not an instant, happy cocoa-bean shade?" I checked my arm. "It looks a little rosy-toned, don't you think?"

"It's the lights in here. Not to mention all the red in the wallpaper. You can't gauge true colors under these lights."

I noticed that while I showered and "tanned," Laurie had drawn the curtains to block the intense afternoon sun. The room was too dark to tell if the bronzing potion was working properly.

"Did you decide which restaurant we should go to?"

"Doesn't matter to me." Laurie responded.

"How about Beachcomber Bob's?" I shook the wrinkles out of the one maternity dress I had brought with me. "That's the one next door, right on the beach with the live music."

"Okay." Laurie headed for the shower, but I didn't think she sounded too convinced Beachcomber Bob's was the spot for us. I wondered if she was disappointed about not going to the luau since this was supposed to be her fancy birthday dinner. I decided I'd ask her about her preference again, once she was out of the bathroom. First, I had an important appointment with my personal salon specialist.

Stepping out on the lanai, I was immersed in sunlight. The evening breeze greeted me with a ruffled hello.

"Swims with dolphins," I said to the wind, as if ordering up my favorite hairstyle by name. All I had to do was sit with my eyes closed and let the invisible fingers do their creative styling with my wet hair.

Basking in the comfort of the moment, I thought of the Hawaiian woman on the beach that morning. She said her song came from Psalm 104. I ducked back inside for my paperback copy of the Psalms and returned to the brilliantly-lit lanai to skim the chapter.

> GOD, my God, how great you are!
> beautifully, gloriously robed,
> Dressed up in sunshine,
> and all heaven stretched out for your tent.
> You built your palace on the ocean deeps,
> made a chariot out of clouds and took off on wind-wings....
> What a wildly wonderful world, GOD!
> You made it all...the deep, wide sea,
> brimming with fish past counting....
> Ships plow those waters....
> All the creatures look expectantly to you....
> You come, and they gather around....
> Send out your Spirit and they spring to life....
> Let GOD enjoy his creation!

Laurie stepped onto the lanai with a towel around her wet hair. "What are you reading?"

"That was fast," I said, surprised.

"You learn to be fast in a house with two bathrooms and four women."

"I was reading Psalm 104 in a contemporary version."

"Is that the 'garlands of hosannas' verse?"

"No, this is the chapter that the woman on the beach this morning said she was singing. Listen to this." I read Laurie the parts I had just skimmed.

As I finished, she said, "Hope, I'm so sorry."

"Sorry? Why? This is beautiful. I wish I'd known what she was saying in Hawaiian when she was singing this."

"I'm sorry because I made fun of you this morning, when you said you thought she was an angel."

"It was the way the light was coming through her white hair," I explained.

"I know, but I thought she was some crazy, Mother-Earth-hugger type of woman when you said she was singing to the ocean."

"No, she was definitely worshiping God. The right God. The only God. You could just tell."

"Read that last line again."

"'Let GOD enjoy his creation.'"

Laurie slowly brushed her hair. "Do you suppose God enjoys us? I mean, I know He loves us and provides for us, but do you think He enjoys us as His artistic creation?"

"I'm sure of it."

"I never considered that before." Laurie lowered her head in quiet contemplation. "It seems that the artwork—the creation—that an artist enjoys are those pieces that mean something personally to him. At least that's how it is with the photographs I enjoy the most. I know it's the same with Gabe. I just never thought of God as enjoying His creation or having parts of it that mean something to Him personally."

"Like us," I added. "Humans seem to be the object of His affection."

"I like that. The object of His affection." Laurie looked out at the ocean. "Would you mind if we didn't go out to any of the touristy restaurants for dinner tonight?"

"No. Whatever you want. You're the birthday girl."

"I'd like to eat dinner right here, just the two of us, with God's huge stage in front of us providing the dinner show."

We ordered a scrumptious dinner complete with coconut cream pie instead of birthday cake. Laurie started a new roll of film and used her remote clicker so she could take shots of both of us while we ate on the lanai, all dressed up, barefoot and wearing our orchid leis looped twice around our heads like birthday crowns.

"Tell me about your new house," I said, as we started in on the pie.

"Potential new house," Laurie corrected me. "It's only a few years old. Something like five thousand square feet."

"Five thousand?"

"I know. It's huge. That's the crazy part. It has four bathrooms. Well, actually, three full baths and a downstairs half bath. Here we spent all those years in a house with two bathrooms, and now that the girls are gone, we're thinking of moving into a mansion."

"Is it a mansion?" I asked. "I mean, would you consider it a mansion?"

"I would, but I don't know if any of the neighbors would. This particular house is small compared to the rest in the area we're looking at. It's on the east side of the bay and has some acreage."

"Do you like the house?"

Laurie's mouth twitched back and forth, as if she were swishing her answer around before spitting it out. "Not really. It's a gorgeous house, and I agree with Gabe that the price is great and the potential is all there. I just don't want to move."

"I can see why that would be hard. You've been in the same house since the day you guys were married. A lot of life is wrapped up in that home."

"Not to mention all the family we have in the immediate area. You know, the more I think about it, Hope, the more resistant I am to moving anywhere. If we were going to make such an upheaval in our lives, we should have done it years ago. Not now. We're too busy to move."

"Even with the girls out of the house?"

"Especially now that the girls are out of the house. And that's another thing." Laurie put down her fork. Her face was turning as red as the wallpaper. "If we were going to move, why didn't we move years ago, when we had three daughters who all wanted their own rooms, not to mention their own bathrooms?"

"No money?" I suggested flippantly.

"Oh, that's right," Laurie said, playing along. "I keep forgetting."

"Do you really? I mean, does it seem as if your life has always been what it is now?"

"Sometimes. I miss the way everything was simple back when we were first married. We had so little money it meant our options were few. Now it seems all we do is have meetings with people who tell us what to do with the money that keeps coming in." Laurie gave a funny little sigh. "I'd complain, but who would feel sorry for me?"

I didn't respond to her quirky statement. Of course I didn't feel sorry for her in the wake of her husband's success. But I still felt for her. I just wasn't sure what I should be feeling.

The sun was about to dip into its evening bath when, from our perch on the eighth floor, Laurie and I heard uproarious laughter coming from the beach below us. We spotted three rather round women, all in long pants and T-shirts, bellowing out the kind of shared laughter that comes from the very bottom of the giggle barrel.

"They must have just arrived," Laurie said.

One of the chortling women went charging into the water, arms first, as if she were going to embrace the entire Pacific with a big kiss. Not to be outdone, the other two women stormed into the salty brine. With supersized squeals followed by supersized splashes, the three of them—clothes and all— were up to their necks in the water.

"What a bunch of sisterchicks!" Laurie exclaimed.

"What did you call them?"

"Sisterchicks. That's what our Realtor called us yesterday when I told her about this trip. Penny said you sounded like the perfect 'sisterchick' to celebrate the big 4-0 with me. She also said she hoped our vacation would be a 'sisterchick adventure' we would never forget."

"That was nice of her. Although, I suppose if we were true sisterchicks, we would be out there with the bobbing Betties."

"But we're wearing dresses," Laurie said. "And we already showered."

"I know. And we just ate."

Silently, from our plush box seats in the balcony, Laurie and I stuffed the last bites of coconut cream pie into our faces and watched the bobbing Betties until the sun disappeared with a faint sizzle. The trio of giddy gals emerged from the water and giggle-hopped their way through the sand, holding up their soggy pant legs. They were such a merry sight.

"Sisterchicks, huh?" I said. "Well, good for them."

"Yes, good for them."

Laurie and I weren't exactly risk takers at the moment. Even the room service pot of coffee we ordered was decaf.

Eleven

The outdoor light on our lanai snapped on automatically in the darkness. Laurie kept looking at my legs.

"What?"

"It's the lighting, I think. It gives you a sort of an amber glow."

I looked at my arm. An orangy stripe was visible on the inside of my arm where the skin was paler. The stripe ran all the way to my palm and along the outside of my thumb.

"It's not turning to a happy, cocoa-bean shade, is it?"

"It's more the shade of an unhappy smashed pumpkin," Laurie said. "But I'm sure it's the light out here."

"I'm going inside to have a look."

Laurie went with me, turning on all the lights. I stood in front of the mirror and made my pathetic declaration. "I'm orange!"

"It's the shadow from the red wallpaper. Try the bathroom mirror."

The bathroom mirror revealed the undeniable truth. I was o-r-a-n-g-e. As o-ran-ge as an orange with a capital O.

Quickly pulling my dress over my head, I stood in front of the mirror in my full slip and examined my disastrous handiwork.

"Oh, Hope! I'm so sorry. I should have helped you. Look at your back."

Across the top of my shoulders were two smeared handprints, evidence of where my fingers had touched my white skin.

"What was I thinking?" I moaned.

"Maybe we can blend it in," Laurie said.

"Why? So I can be orange all over? No thanks. I have to figure out how to wash off this stuff. What if I take a long soak in the bathtub?"

"It's worth a try." Laurie lifted the edge of my flippy hairdo to reveal strangely striped skin on my ear and neck, proof of exactly where my hand had trailed the lotion. It looked as if I had purposefully drawn a row of lines down my neck.

"I look like a Dreamsicle," I groaned. "You know, those Popsicles with orange on the outside and vanilla ice cream on the inside? That's what I look like."

"I have some facial scrub." Laurie rummaged in her cosmetic bag. "Why don't you take a long soak and try using this, especially on your neck."

It was a good idea. But the results were less than encouraging. The longer I soaked, the murkier the water became. If I'd been thinking clearly, I would have drained the water several times rather than sitting in it and letting the diluted color continue to permeate my skin.

But then, if I had been thinking clearly, I wouldn't have bought the bargain brand. Or more specifically, I wouldn't have bought any brand of fake tan. I would have been content with my skin color.

"It's a lesson in vanity," I said with a self-pitying sniff, as I crawled into bed. I hid my legs under the covers because they clashed with the bedspread. "You said the beauty years are over at forty, right? I guess I'm going out with a bang then. A big, tangerine starburst sort of bang."

"Do you need some Oreos?" Laurie asked sympathetically. "I could buy some. And some Reese's Pieces, too, if it would help."

"No, I'm too full. Besides, we're both in bed already."

"Maybe in the morning you can take another shower and—"

"And what? Scrape off the top layer of my epidermis with my fingernails?"

"Not with your fingernails. We could get you one of those loofah sponges. The color only tints the top of your skin, right?"

"One would hope."

"I feel so bad for talking you into this."

"Hey, I went along with it wholeheartedly, Laurie, so don't blame yourself. I'm the one who tried to get a bargain and bought the cheaper brand."

"The more expensive brand might have had a worse effect. Who knows? You have delicate skin. We should have thought of that."

"And I'm pregnant. Don't forget how the hormone factor taints everything."

"Maybe there's such a thing as skin bleach."

"Laurie, I know you mean well, but I think I'm done talking about this. I'll live. We'll laugh about it really hard sometime. But not right now. My body is still on East Coast time, and I'm fried. I'm going to sleep."

I closed my eyes, half expecting to dream about being a runaway Popsicle that gallivanted into the ocean and floated around on a big, blue bubble-belly. However, I have no idea if that's what I dreamed about because I was too dead asleep to remember.

Laurie and I woke to the sound of rain. Not gentle, pitter-patter rain, but buckets and buckets of the wet stuff that dashed against the sliding door to the lanai. We couldn't believe we were looking out on the same landscape that had lulled us with its soothing beauty the day before.

"No pohuehue today." I stood barefoot by the window and wished I had brought my big, fuzzy slippers with me.

Laurie didn't hear me. She was pulling on her clothes.

"Where are you going?"

"To the gift shop. Do you want anything?"

"No, thanks. Would you like me to order some breakfast? I was thinking we could split an omelette."

"Good idea. Nothing with bell peppers or onions, though."

"Right, I remember you don't like those." As soon as Laurie was out the door, I called room service and ordered a three-cheese omelette, fruit salad, and a Danish instead of the toast.

Slipping back under the covers, I stared out the window, wistfully recalling the glory of yesterday's walk on the beach. This morning the only bright, golden glow seemed to be the one coming from my skin.

I stumbled to the bathroom and had a good look. I was still orange. Still streaked. So sad.

I looked at all of Laurie's cosmetics lined up on the right side of the bathroom counter. She still used the same brand of contact lens solution she had in college. Her toothpaste tube was folded neatly at the bottom and rolled up with the cap securely in place.

I can't explain the sweet comfort I felt as I surveyed the lineup. The cosmetics represented a logical, Laurie-order in a world in which a grown woman could declare she was comfortable in her own skin at lunchtime and yet turn herself orange a few hours later.

For one insane moment, I thought of trying her nail polish remover—not on my face, just on the insides of my arms.

Blessedly, Laurie returned at that insane moment. "I bought a few things for you." She pulled some lemon juice, a bottle of bath oil, and a pastel pink scrubber from her bag.

"You didn't have to do that."

"Yes, I did. I think the lemon juice will be a good natural bleach. Another long soak with this softening oil might make that top layer easier to rub off. Did you order breakfast?"

"Yes."

"I picked up a coffee at the espresso cart in the lobby. I didn't buy you anything because I wasn't sure what you're drinking these days. I could go back and get you chai or a steamer."

"That's okay. Thanks anyway. I'll make some tea."

Laurie looked out at the wet world beyond our lanai. "Tropical rainstorms are kind of spooky, don't you think? It reminds me of *Key Largo,* being caught on this little island and not being able to get off it because of the weather, but you're not cold. Everything is still open to the air and balmy, but it's wet everywhere."

"I didn't know you had been to Key Largo."

"I haven't. I'm talking about the movie. With Humphrey Bogart. You remember how the hurricane came through and ransacked the hotel?"

"No."

"How did you go through childhood without seeing all the great oldies?"

"Unlike you, I didn't have an uncle who ran the only movie theater in town."

"Oh, right. I had an advantage there, didn't I? By the way, I noticed an activities list in the elevator. The hotel offers a lei-making class today."

A knock on our door was followed by the welcome words, "Room service." I hid in the bathroom while Laurie answered. We ate on our beds like a couple of little girls kept home from school due to sniffles on a rainy day.

Once I slipped into the bathtub, I doused myself in lemon juice, soaking long and scrubbing hard. It actually worked.

At least that's what Laurie concurred, when she examined my legs and arms with me in the filtered daylight that came through our closed sliding glass door. She said I had gone from an acorn squash shade of orange to something closer to a cantaloupe tone. I decided it was an improvement and I shouldn't think about it anymore.

"We should start a list of possible indoor activities for today," Laurie said. "I need to buy some new sandals or at least some flip-flops. I checked the gift shop downstairs, but they don't have what I need."

"Maybe we could find somewhere to go for tea this afternoon," I said.

"Sure. And what about the lei-making class?"

"Good idea." I put on a pair of long pants and a long-sleeved cotton shirt and felt like I'd covered up enough of the orange skin so as not to shock anyone once we got out in public. The faded lines along my neck were still a bit exotic, though.

"What if I tried wearing a bandana around my neck, the

way the girl on the catamaran did yesterday?"

"You could try it," Laurie said cautiously.

"I know; it wouldn't quite have the same effect, would it?"

"Probably not."

Laurie threw a few items in her straw beach bag, and we headed down to the hotel lobby in search of the lei class. We noticed an older woman in a mu'umu'u, seated at a table in an outdoor shaded alcove. The table was spread with a variety of colorful flowers. She looked up as Laurie and I approached and said, "*Aloha. E como mai.* Welcome."

I knew that voice immediately. It was the gentle woman from the beach. She had welcomed my first morning on the island with a song, and now she was welcoming us to her table.

"Good morning," I greeted her bashfully.

The woman smiled at me. She remembered me.

I smiled back. Our gaze into each other's eyes remained fixed.

"May we join you?" Laurie flashed a broad grin in my direction. I knew she had figured out the special connection I had with this woman.

"Yes, please. Sit. I am Kapuna Kalala."

We introduced ourselves and pulled out the folding chairs, sitting at the table covered with a floral feast.

"These are beautiful flowers," Laurie said. "I love the purple orchids. They're so intricate."

"Yes," the woman said. "The vanda orchids are sewn into the lei faceup to show their beauty."

Handing each of us a needle that was nearly a foot long and threaded with smooth, white string, Kapuna Kalala showed us how to select the strongest flowers and where to pierce them with the needle so they would receive the least amount of damage.

Her weathered, brown hands passed over the delicate flowers, reaching for the purest white tuberose blooms and holding them out to me. *"Ona, ona,"* she chanted. "That means to breathe in and smell the sweetness."

I bent closer to the tiny tuberose. They looked like little firecrackers that had exploded, leaving one end frayed. With the explosion came the most intoxicating fragrance I had ever smelled. "Oh, that's amazing."

She explained how all the white flowers, such as gardenias, tuberose, and plumeria, bruise easily and turn brown, but the smaller pink plumeria last longer.

"Such as this *pikake*." She twirled a dainty blossom of jasmine between her gnarled fingers. "We use this flower for leis when the occasion is special. Especially for brides. I do not have the maile leaf to show you. The maile leaf is used for a lei that is worn like a long sash around the neck."

"Are we supposed to string these in a specific order?" Laurie asked.

"Yes."

"What order?"

"That depends." Kapuna Kalala tilted her head. "What is your story?"

Twelve

My story?" Laurie asked.

"Every lei is an expression. It reveals much about the one who made it. What do you want to say with your creation? What do you want to say to the person who will receive it? When you know that, you will know how to string your lei."

Laurie didn't require any further art direction. All her creative juices flowed into her work with a passion.

I thought about art and passion and creation. Did God string together the events of our lives based on what He wanted to reveal about Himself? Or do we get halfway through life like this and start to notice that a story exists that He has wanted to tell through the order of events?

The thought was too cumbersome for such a moment as this. I put my needle aside and rummaged for Laurie's camera so I could capture this moment. I wanted Laurie to go home with proof that, when given an opportunity to create, she was passionate.

Our knowledgeable instructor continued to talk while I took pictures of the two of them and the assortment of gorgeous flowers.

"To the ancient Hawaiians, the adornment of the body was an important way to display their artistic expression," she said. "They used feathers, ivory, beads, shells, flowers, leaves…"

Kapuna Kalala dropped her sentence as she concentrated on the lei in her hands and picked up a new thought. "Do you see how I am finishing this off? This is the *kipu'u* of lei making—the knotting. You are doing the *ku'l*—the stringing. The more complicated leis involve *wili, hili,* and *humupapa.*"

She chuckled at the rhyming sound of her own words. "Those are the winding, braiding, and sewing. But I am starting you off easy with your first one. The ones with more winding and braiding are more complicated, but they are also more beautiful."

For a moment I had to remind myself she was talking about leis, not about complicated lives. Although the truth seemed to apply to both.

I was so enjoying listening to Kapuna Kalala's lulling voice and taking pictures of Laurie as she let loose with all her creative energies that I didn't jump into my lei making. I was having more fun watching, so I tucked a pink plumeria behind my ear and took a few more photos.

"Can you say *pua?*"

Laurie and I both tried.

"This is our word for 'flower.' Sometimes children are affectionately called *pua* because they are fragile and sweet and small. They stay with us for such a short time. Think of this the next time a child links his arms around your neck and you wear his embrace like a lei."

I sat spellbound by the wisdom in her words.

Laurie sat hunched over, finishing her creation. She had carefully strung one tender pink rosebud after every four tuberose all the way around her lei. At the beginning and at the end she had fastened a stunning purple orchid. Both of the orchids were fastened properly, with their faces forward. When Kapuna Kalala showed Laurie how to knot them together, the vanda orchids looked like twins growing out of the same stem.

Turning to me with a radiant expression, Laurie said, "Hope, I made this for you. This is your story. Do you see? Between the firecrackers I tucked a little pink Emilee Rose, and I anchored the circle with two rare beauties facing forward. That's us. You know who the four firecrackers are."

I could barely move. It was so beautiful. This work of art was my story.

"Laurie…"

No other words followed. I leaned over and kissed her on the cheek. She slipped the lei over my bowed head.

"*Aloha*," Kapuna Kalala said. "*Aloha nui loa.* With much love." Coming from her deep voice, the words sounded as if they were rising like an ocean swell.

Laurie picked up the camera and took a picture of me, sitting there, speechless, with my story adorning my neck like a garland of hosannas.

Now that Laurie had the camera, she redirected her passion. Kapuna Kalala continued her lesson for us, appearing unaffected by Laurie's picture taking.

"Hawaiians love to talk story. We love to give story. Every lei holds a story, and everyone who wears a lei holds on to that story."

"How did you learn to make leis?" I asked.

"From my mother. She used to make flower leis and sell them to the tourists who came in on the ships at the Aloha Tower. Sometimes she would spend two hours making a lei and sell it for one dollar. Then she would watch the ship go out to sea, and the people would throw the lei into the water."

"I've heard of that tradition," Laurie said. "If the lei floated back to you, didn't that mean you were supposed to return to the islands one day?"

A patient smile played on Kapuna Kalala's lips. "Yes, but this is not a Hawaiian tradition. A Hawaiian would not throw away something that was made for her. She would not toss aside one gift to wish for another."

Kapuna Kalala held up the lei she had finished. Using both hands, she held it gingerly, the way one would hold a special treasure.

"In ancient times, leis were used in worship. Now that I

know the true God and Creator of all, I always offer up to Him the fragrance, which is the firstfruits of my gift."

She held the lei silently for a moment. Laurie snapped a picture. I wished she had used her digital camera because that one wouldn't have made a noise and interrupted the sacred moment.

The rain started coming down furiously, and the wind blew sheets of water into the alcove where we were seated. Laurie quickly covered her camera, and the three of us scampered to gather up everything of value and move deeper into the hotel lobby. Our lei-making lesson had come to an abrupt conclusion.

"Thank you." I placed my hand on Kapuna Kalala's shoulder. "Thank you so much. Thank you for the song yesterday morning and thank you for the lesson today."

"*Ho'omaika'i.*" She looked at me tenderly. "Blessings on you. *He Akua Hemolele.*"

"What does that phrase mean? You sang it yesterday."

"It means 'God is holy or perfect.'" The dear woman reached over and lightly touched my abdomen. "May I say a *pule* for you and your baby?"

I nodded, even though I wasn't sure what a "poo-lay" was. I guessed it was a blessing or a prayer.

Drawing in a deep breath, she leaned close and breathed out the heart-melting words, whose sound I was beginning to adore. "*Ka Makua-O-Kalani. Mahalo, mahalo.*" The words came out carefully strung together, cascading from her lips like an exquisite and fragrant lei, encircling Emilee Rose and me.

"Thank you. Thank you so much." I listened to my own voice and hated the small, tight, nasal sound of my words compared to hers. I didn't know until that moment that the English language doesn't easily melt or soothe the soul.

Laurie didn't say anything until we were through the lobby and standing in front of the elevator. "That was incredible."

"Yes, it was."

"What are we doing now?"

"I don't know."

The rain had knocked out any possibility of outdoor activities, and our amazing time with Kapuna Kalala had put both Laurie and me into a stupor, not knowing where to go next.

"Shopping?" I suggested.

"You wanted to visit a teahouse, right? We could find a place now for lunch; it's a good day for tea. Let's go up to the room so I can grab a sweater."

I decided to leave Laurie's special lei in our room. I didn't want to wear it in the rain and watch it disintegrate. We checked with the concierge, and he recommended the Winterbourne Tea Parlor at the Mission Houses Museum for our rainy-day tea. Sliding into a cab, Laurie and I rode through the dense traffic on soggy Kalakaua Avenue.

We had only gone about three blocks when Laurie said, "Wait! Stop the car. Is that the Wilson Roberts Gallery?"

"Yes, that's the main one," the taxi driver said. "There's another one at the Ala Moana Shopping Center."

"This is the one I want. Could you let us out here at the

corner?" She pulled a few dollars from her wallet to pay him for the short ride.

I followed Laurie, not sure what was going on. "I'm guessing this has something to do with art or with Gabe," I said, as we hurried from the cab into the gallery.

"Right there," Laurie said quietly. She nodded at an entire wall filled with Gabe's artwork. Across the top of the paintings reigned a sign in gold and black that read, "Gabriel Giordani— Painter of Hideaways."

I stood in silent appreciation. They were beautiful paintings. All of them. Gabriel often painted vine-covered cottages or garden scenes, but what set his work apart from others was that each of his paintings included a subtle "hideaway" that was just the right size for children. Some paintings showed a tree house or a playhouse discreetly hidden to the side. In his more recent works he had painted pint-sized, fortlike hideaways that appeared to have been created out of cedar branches by an imaginative eight-year-old. The unspoken message of each painting was that a child had just been there, innocently at play, in the imaginary castle or impenetrable fortress of twigs.

Laurie stood close and whispered, "Gabe told me to try to stop in at one of their locations while we were here. They just started to carry his work a few months ago."

"It's really wonderful, Laurie."

She looked wary as a young couple stopped in front of Gabe's largest painting.

In a rather high-pitched voice, the young woman said, "I don't get the big attraction. I mean, why is his stuff everywhere?"

"He's Italian," the guy said.

I could feel Laurie cringe.

"I know, but who keeps buying his pictures?"

"People who enjoy financing his villa in Rome."

"Seriously, doesn't the American public realize this kind of nostalgia is nauseating?"

"Or at best annoying," he agreed.

I began to take a step forward when Laurie grabbed my arm. "Art is subjective," she muttered under her breath. "Everyone is entitled to his or her own opinion. Didn't you remind me of that yesterday?"

"Yes, but—"

The young woman spoke again. "He obviously isn't in touch with what speaks to the postmodern generation. I think this Italian guy should go back to art school."

"He's probably too busy living the life of a capitalistic playboy," the guy said.

That does it!

Holding up my index finger, I scrunched up my nose and said, "Just one minute, Laurie. I'll be right back."

"Hello there." I approached the opinionated couple as if I owned the gallery.

"Not buying. Just looking," the curt young man said.

"I'm not employed here." I tried to keep my voice low and

controlled. "I happened to overhear some of your comments, and I just wanted you to know that your assumptions about Gabriel Giordani are all wrong. Terribly wrong. Completely. Just wrong."

The couple looked at my set expression, then down at my belly and back at my faintly orange-tinted face with the exotic stripes running across my neck. I'm sure they had never seen such an extraordinary combination of guts and glamour.

I was not to be deterred. "Gabriel Giordani does not live in a villa in Italy. He is an American. Third generation. He and his family have lived in the same three-bedroom house for almost twenty years and—"

"Do you really know him?" The woman's interest was piqued. "Have you actually been to his house?"

"Yes."

Two more rainy-day gallery strollers stepped close. Laurie had withdrawn to the corner of the room and was trying to appear interested in a sculpture of a barnacle-crusted blue whale. I caught every cautionary expression she sent my way, but that didn't stop me.

"How did you meet him?" a woman wearing a purple visor asked.

"I met him when I was in college," I answered. "I worked at a restaurant, and he used to come in. Often."

"How fascinating! What is he really like? I've seen pictures, and he's very handsome."

"Yes, well, he's a wonderful man and..." I raised my voice but not my gaze, "he has a really wonderful wife and family."

"Does he ever give you any of his paintings?" the purple-billed woman asked.

"No."

"Too bad. They're worth a lot, you know," the young man said.

"No kidding!" his wife agreed. "If you had some of his earlier works and if he had signed them back then, can you imagine what they would be worth now on eBay?"

The purple visor looked at me closely. "Do you really know him personally, or did you just meet him once?"

"No, he's a good friend."

"And he never gave you one of his paintings?"

I couldn't believe how smothered I felt. I had boldly stepped forward in an effort to defend Gabe and protect Laurie, but now I was defending myself. The reason I had never accepted one of Gabe's offers of a painting was because Darren and I agreed we didn't want to appear as if we were abusing our friendship. But I wasn't going to explain that to this mob.

A salesman suddenly appeared and stepped up to do his job. I've never been so thankful for an aggressive salesman as I was at that moment.

Making my exit, I found Laurie waiting in the corner of the gallery. "Sorry about that. I thought I was being so noble."

"I know. It's okay. Let's just get out of here."

I followed Laurie out to the street where she hailed a cab.

"Winterbourne Tea Parlor," she said. "At the Mission Houses Museum."

"Certainly," the driver said. "And how is your day going?"

Laurie and I looked at each other. Neither of us seemed to know what to say.

Thirteen

Another bucket of water tipped over and spilled from the heavens. Gigantic blobs of rain pelted the cab's roof as the vehicle sloshed its way through the Honolulu streets.

"I appreciate what you tried to do back there, defending my husband like that," Laurie said quietly.

"It didn't go the way I thought it would."

"Don't worry about it."

"I can see what you meant yesterday about opening yourself up for criticism when you put your art on display. It can be brutal."

"Yes, but so is giving birth to a baby—any baby. You were right, Hope. You said I have to just give birth and trust God for the rest."

"Did I say that?"

"Yes, you did. See? I told you the wisdom would roll in as soon as you turned forty."

"Don't rush me. I still have a few more days in the season of beauty. "

Laurie looked out the window and back at me. "Maybe you're getting a jump start on the wisdom era because I've been thinking a lot about what you said. I've been carrying around this 259-pound baby for too long."

"So what are you going to do?"

"I'm not sure."

"If you start having contractions, I'm here for you. You know that. I'd love to be your midwife and get this baby out of you."

Laurie grinned and nudged me with her elbow. I looked up and saw the driver giving the two of us the strangest looks in his rearview mirror.

"Don't worry," Laurie said more for his benefit than mine. "I don't plan to go into labor right away. At least not today."

"Me neither," I said, trying to offer him double reassurance.

The driver pulled up in front of a low stone wall and pointed to the amount due on his meter. I handed Laurie some money and peered out the window. The rain had subsided temporarily, and I had a clear view of a lovely, white two-story clapboard house that graced the center of the grounds. It was as if a bit of New England had popped up in the middle of this tropical island. Mature trees sheltered this charming frame house and adjacent buildings, making it feel like an oasis in the center of the city.

"Do you know who built this house?" I asked the driver.

"The Protestant missionaries." He turned and looked at me, as if checking to see if I wanted more information.

"Do you happen to know when it was built?" Turning to Laurie I added, "Doesn't it look like the house across the street from the Ladybug?"

"It does," Laurie said.

"In the mid-1800s," the driver said. "It arrived from Boston board by board, shipped around Cape Horn. One of the missionary families who lived here taught a school for the *keiki* of the *alii.*"

"A school for whom?" Laurie asked, combining our cash to pay him.

"The children of the Hawaiian royalty. My wife's great, great aunt was Lili'uokalani." He paused, waiting for us to be impressed, but of course, we were beggars when it came to Hawaiian history.

I asked for a little more.

"Lili'uokalani was the last reigning monarch of Hawai'i. The teacher who lived in this house taught Lili'uokalani to play the piano when she was only three years old. The teacher's name was Juliette Cooke, as in Castle and Cooke."

Again, we were sadly uninformed.

"Lili'uokalani wrote hundreds of songs. Have you ever heard of 'Aloha Oe'?" He started to sing for us in a mellow voice.

"Yes," Laurie and I said in unison.

"She was my wife's great, great aunt," he stated again

proudly. Nodding to the frame house he added, "I don't know what they tell you on the tour in there, but not all the missionaries who came here were haoles."

As we emerged from the cab, I noticed that the sun had found a tiny crevice in the overhead lake of clouds and had let down a thin golden line, fishing around for admirers. I swished across the wet pavement, ready to bite on the shimmering hook.

Zip. With a snap, the golden line was retracted, and we were left with wet feet.

"What was that word the driver used?" Laurie asked.

"Haole?"

"Yes. Where did we hear that before?"

I refreshed her memory on how the one-eyed hotel *mauka* mama had called me that and then the bandana girl on the catamaran explained that it wasn't a compliment.

"Right, but didn't the guy on the catamaran say it meant 'no breath'?" Laurie asked.

"That's right. He did. So what does that mean? Not all the missionaries who came here had 'no breath.'" I shrugged.

We followed the pavement around to the covered portico in front of the Mission Houses Museum gift shop. A bearded gentleman standing behind a counter under the green roof greeted us with "Aloha" and asked if we were there for the tour.

"Actually, we're going to the tea parlor," Laurie said.

"You're almost there." He motioned to his right. "The Winterbourne Tea Parlor is around the corner of the gift shop. You can't miss it."

For some reason I assumed the tea parlor would be inside the white house, the same way it was set up at the Ladybug Tea and Cakes that I ran at home with my neighbor Sharla. "You don't serve tea in the frame house?" I asked.

"No. We offer tours, though, up until four o'clock this afternoon."

A tour sounded like the perfect rainy day activity to me, but I wasn't sure if Laurie would feel the same. I knew she was set on finding a new pair of sandals before the day was over.

Our luncheon at the Winterbourne Tea Parlor was scrumptious and relaxing. Laurie and I sat at a small table beneath a quilt hung on the wall as art. The sign below the quilt said it was the Hawaiian breadfruit pattern. I liked the English china sugar bowl on the table. The old Hawaiian elements seemed to have found a way to blend with the European encroachments upon this island in a peaceful manner inside this quiet haven.

As I popped the last bite of scone smothered in guava jelly into my mouth, I overheard two of the other guests talking about the tour they had just taken of the Mission Houses.

"This is a wonderful place," I said to the young woman who slipped the check on the corner of our table and asked if she could bring us anything else.

Laurie slapped her credit card on the check before I could reach for my purse. Then, as if to explain my appreciation for all things tea-ish, Laurie added, "My friend here owns a tea-house in New England."

"You do? Where is it?"

"Connecticut."

"Really? I'm going to Connecticut this spring for my brother's college graduation. Maybe I can come by for a visit to your shop."

"You should," Laurie said. "It's in Hartford. You'll love it. They fixed up an old house, and all the visitors love to stop by there after the tours."

Laurie had left out some helpful details so I explained further. "The Ladybug is in an area called Nook Farm. The Mark Twain house and Harriet Beecher Stowe house are right there, open for tours, and that's how my neighbor got the idea that we should start a teahouse. Visitors take the tours, and then they want to sit and eat and talk about it."

"That sounds similar to what it's like here at the Winterbourne," the waitress said. "Do you happen to have a business card?"

"No, I didn't bring any with me. But I can write down the information, if you want."

"Yes, please. I'll get you some paper and one of our cards."

She returned with another woman, who shook my hand and introduced herself as the tutu of the Winterbourne Parlor. I remembered from the pigtailed twins I saw at baggage claim that a tutu was a grandma or an elderly person.

"May I ask you a question?" the tutu said. "Do you order your loose leaf tea from the mainland, or do you have to use an international source? I ask because we've been having some problems with our distributor lately."

"We work with an excellent company on the West Coast. Have you heard of the Carnelian Rose Tea Company?"

She shook her head.

"I don't have their information with me, but they have managed to get us any kind of tea we want. Ask for Jennifer. She's wonderful."

"Good. I'll look up their website and contact Jennifer," the tutu said. "We are having difficulty ordering the Madame Butterfly tea, and we need it for a big event next month."

"I know Jennifer carries Madame Butterfly." Turning to Laurie I explained. "It's a green jasmine tea. Very smooth. Each of the leaves is rolled up by hand, and when they get agonized in the boiling water, they unfurl like butterfly wings."

Laurie smiled at my passionate description and then looked at the two women standing by our table. "I'm a die-hard coffee drinker, but she's always trying to convert me. Give me a nice, dark Arabica Italian roast in a double brevé latte or a doppio cappuccino any morning, and I'm good to go all day."

The three of us looked at Laurie as if she were speaking a foreign language.

"Although," she added quickly, "I do enjoy the Ladybug signature blend tea. Jennifer created that one for the grand opening of the Ladybug Tea and Cakes, didn't she, Hope?"

"Yes, she did."

Laurie seemed to be trying hard to prove that she could hold her own in the world of tea talk. "I love the Ladybug blend, which has a yummy vanilla, sugar-cookie taste. That's a good one as well as the chocolate mint tea, which is stronger. More full bodied."

"Chocolate mint tea?" The tutu looked at the young waitress, who gave an approving nod. "Now that would do very well around here with some of our regular customers."

"They must be sisterchicks then," Laurie said. "Because my Realtor, Penny Lane, told me that no sisterchick can pass up really good chocolate."

I gave her a little kick under the table and a look that said, *You can stop now. We'll let you stay in the good graces of the tea circle. Just stop talking now. Please.*

When the ladies walked away from the table, Laurie leaned over and whispered, "Why did you kick me?"

"Oh, did I kick you?" I replied with an innocent smirk. "So sorry."

"Was I embarrassing you?"

"You? Never." My grin widened. "You make me smile, you little brevé, full-bodied, Arabica sisterchick, you."

Laurie responded with a comical grin that showed all her front teeth and none of her lips.

I laughed. "I haven't seen that silly grin on you for a long time."

"Stick around. I think I have a few more of those bubbling up to the surface."

"Always good to know that we bring out the best in each other, isn't it?"

"Nothing but the best. Besides, it drives Gabe crazy when I make that face. I have to get all of them out of my system this week before I go home."

The waitress returned with the credit card and held it for a moment. "Is this your real name?"

I watched Laurie shrink an inch and fold her shoulders in toward her chest. "Yes," she answered in a thin voice. "I'm Laurinda Giordani."

"Wow, really. That is so amazing," the young woman said.

All my protective-instinct feathers started to ruffle. If this woman was about to ask for Laurie to get her Gabe's autograph or ask him to donate a free painting to their tea parlor, I was ready to squawk nice and loud.

"I have a cousin named Laurinda," she said. "I've never met another Laurinda. I think it's a beautiful name."

Laurie paused a moment before realizing that the Giordani part of her name wasn't factoring into this conversation. "Thank you," she said, nodding gracefully.

The two of us exchanged knowing glances as we got up to leave. The incognito princess had managed to visit an art gallery and dine on scones and guava jelly without being detected. Two for two. I wondered if we could complete this day with a perfect score.

Fourteen

Next item of business—shopping for shoes." Laurie was heading toward the street and looking for the nearest cab to hail. The clouds above were sifting out a fine mist that made me feel like an overly attended-to house fern.

"What about the Mission Houses tour?" I asked.

"Did you really want to go on the tour?"

I was about to say, "Not unless you do," but then I realized that wouldn't be the truth. I really wanted to go on the tour. I wanted to see the inside of the house. I was curious if they had the actual piano on display that the missionary teacher had used to instruct three-year-old Lili'uokalani.

"Yes." I stopped under a sheltering tree. "I would really like to go on the tour."

"Oh, okay." Laurie turned around and headed back toward the information desk. I watched her feet trekking through the puddles in her strappy sandals and knew that those prissy little darlings were not going to be happy much longer.

"Wait," I said, remaining under the tree. "Let's talk about this."

I had been trained over the years by my male shopping companions that the objective of going to the mall was to seek the needed item, snag it, bag it, and bring it home for dinner. That's why I started to shop by catalog.

Laurie, however, had spent the past two decades turning mall meandering into an art form with her daughters. It was better that she take on the shops by herself and I take on the tour with only Emilee Rose to think about.

Laurie had joined me under the tree.

"We don't both have to go on the tour," I said. "Why don't you go shopping and meet me back here in a couple of hours? If I finish the tour and you're not back yet, I'll poke around in the gift shop or have another cup of tea."

"Are you sure?"

"Fly. Be free. Find some new sandals. I don't think it would be fair to my pudgy sausage feet if I subjected them to viewing all the sleek little numbers available in Honolulu and then told my feet they couldn't take any of the shoes home with them."

"You're sure you don't mind doing it this way?"

"Positive."

"Okay. I'll be back in a couple of hours. Keep your cell phone on."

I bought my ticket and had just enough time for a visit to

the little girls' room before the next tour.

"If you can imagine," the tour guide said, starting us off in the primitive kitchen. "Juliette and her husband raised their own seven children while providing room, board, and private schooling for, at one point, as many as sixteen royal children. The Royal School wasn't started on this property, but Juliette lived in this house for more than forty years."

I realized he was talking about the teacher that the cab driver had mentioned.

"Listen to what Juliette wrote in a letter home to the good people of Sunderland, Massachusetts, in 1842."

I smiled. I knew where Sunderland was. We had even driven through there once on our way home from a wedding in Amherst.

Last night I had the King and Chiefs here to tea. Chiefs always expect cake, and nice cake too. I had bread and butter, cup cakes, cookies, fried cakes, sponge cake, crackers, cheese, tea and coffee. I used 40 eggs in my cookery, and the board was swept clean. Now I must express in plain language that the expense of this entertainment was borne by the Chiefs and not the Mission lest you might wonder if it was right for Missionaries thus to appropriate the money given them for the spreading of the Blessed Gospel. His Majesty was in excellent spirit. His wife is a very pretty native, a professed Christian. All present appeared to enjoy the evening.

My heart went out to this missionary woman. She seemed like a kindred spirit. All Juliette was trying to do was serve a nice little tea. I knew what that was like. *I guess it doesn't matter how you're expressing yourself creatively. There's always someone who will criticize your attempt.*

Inside the main living area I noticed a small piano, and I asked if that was the one Juliette had used to teach the students. The guide seemed impressed with my question but didn't have an answer. He wasn't sure if the piano belonged to the Cooke family or if it had belonged to the Chamberlains, the first missionary family to occupy this house.

The tour moved on to a tiny building next door on the mission compound. The coral-block room contained a working replica of the original printing press.

"The first translated portion of Holy Scripture was the one-hundredth psalm," the guide explained. "It was in leaflet form and distributed at the dedication of the Kawaiaha'o Church, the large, coral-block sanctuary, which you've certainly noticed right across the street."

As I was thinking that I had probably missed seeing the church because of the downpour, the tour guide held up a sample sheet of printed paper. "It took fifteen years to translate the entire Bible into Hawaiian because, of course, before the Protestant missionaries arrived, the Hawaiian people had no written language."

It was easy to see why the Hawaiian Bible he then held up was so thick. The Hawaiian alphabet, he explained, contained only twelve letters. Some of the words were excessively long, and many of the phrases took several words to express.

"For example," he said, "the book *Pilgrim's Progress* was printed here, and the title in Hawaiian is *Ka Hele Malihini 'ana mai Kela Ao aku a Kela Ao*."

The others in the small tour group chuckled, but I wished the guide would read some of the Bible to us so we could hear the words roll off the whitewashed walls in that tiny, hallowed printing room. I wanted to hear more of God's Word in Hawaiian to find out if it sounded as rich and filling as Kapuna Kalala's words.

After the tour, I took my time strolling through the gift shop. I browsed through the extensive and beautiful books on the shelves and picked up one about Juliette because I was curious to know more about her.

On a table in the center of the room, I noticed a small, purse-sized oval mirror in a deep, smooth wood. The label on the back identified the wood as koa. I had never heard of koa wood, but I loved the feel. I held the mirror in my hand for a long time before deciding to buy it.

The timing was perfect because Laurie pulled up in a cab and motioned for the driver to wait while she hopped out and entered the gift shop.

"Do you need more time?" she asked.

"No, I'm ready."

We climbed into the taxi's backseat, and I pushed aside several bags. "Looks like you did well."

"I did. I found two pairs of sandals that are both exactly what I needed. And look at this." She pulled a Bible from one of her bags. "I found one just like yours at a Christian bookstore at the shopping center. Only this one is the whole Bible and not just Psalms."

I reached for the thick book and turned to Psalm 100.

"What are you looking up?"

"Something I learned on the tour. This is the first portion of Scripture that was translated into Hawaiian. Should I read it aloud?"

"Of course."

I read the chapter to her starting with:

On your feet now—applaud GOD!
Bring a gift of laughter,
sing yourselves into his presence.

I looked over at Laurie. Her eyes were glistening.

"That is so fresh. Hope, do you suppose it sounded that rich and inviting to the people here the first time they heard it?"

"Better," I said. "They heard it in Hawaiian."

Gazing out the cab's window, I noticed that the sun was making a late afternoon appearance and bossing the breeze around, telling it where to go sweep up the puddles before closing time. I wondered how fast the trade winds felt like working on what had previously seemed like their day off.

Returning to the hotel, we found our evening luau had

been canceled due to the heavy rains. The water wasn't drying quickly enough to guarantee dry seating on the grass mats at the outdoor luau. After much debate, Laurie and I decided to go ahead and make a reservation for one of the indoor luaus and not wait another night, just in case the weather didn't cooperate tomorrow, either.

"Besides," I told Laurie, "I'm better off in a chair. I'm not sure how I would manage to sit on a straw mat and then get up in any sort of dainty fashion."

"I must remind myself how proper you've become ever since you moved to New England."

"Proper? Me? Ha! Guess again. And for the record, I'm not sure any of my neighbors would consider me a New Englander. I've only lived there for, what? Seventeen years? I'm still a visitor to them."

Laurie shook her head. "You don't realize it, but the New Englander in you shows in the little things like the way you flatten out your A's sometimes at the ends of your sentences or the way you sit in a restaurant. You're definitely a Connecticut Yankee. They're your people now."

I thought about what Laurie said while we got ready for the luau. During the tour, the guide said that Juliette set sail from Boston when she was twenty-four and spent the rest of her life in Honolulu, passing away at the age of eighty-four. She certainly wasn't a tourist. Not a visitor. Hawai'i was her home for sixty years. Had the Hawaiians truly become her people?

Laurie wore the cutest capri outfit to the luau. She had a hard time deciding between the two new pairs of sandals. I talked her into wearing the ones with the low heel because we planned to walk to a neighboring hotel for the luau.

We entered a banquet-style room where rows of tables were set with festive colors with a bowl of pineapples and papayas in the center. We signed in and were given a choice of a lei made of plastic shells or a lei made of plastic flowers.

After the amazing experience Laurie and I had that morning with Kapuna Kalala, I couldn't bear to even look at the plastic flower leis. Apparently Laurie couldn't either because we both deferred to the plastic shell leis. Fashionable Laurie wrapped hers around her wrist a few times and wore it as a bracelet.

We chose two chairs at a table near the front. I sat down while Laurie went to get us some tropical punch.

Slack key guitar music floated through the room as a large, boisterous group entered, ready for a good time. One of the younger girls from the group gravitated away from the rest and came over to the table where I waited for Laurie.

"Is anyone sitting here?" She pointed to the chair across from me.

"No." I glanced at the rest of the group, secretly hoping they wouldn't join her.

"Are you by yourself?" I asked.

"I'm trying to be," she said in a low voice. Looking over her shoulder she added, "I'm here for a dinner with my company.

It's our annual sales conference. But I would have stayed in my room if they would have let me."

She had warm, brown skin and expressive, dark eyes. I was surprised at how open she seemed. Maybe I was the closest thing to a motherly figure in the room, and she felt safe with me.

"Are you okay?" I asked, knowing that she could take that any way she wanted. If some weasel was stalking her at this company picnic, I could give her a few tips on self-defense. However, if she merely felt a headache coming on, I could recommend a little sip of fruit punch to bring up her blood sugar.

"Yeah, I'm okay." She looked around again and then said, "I grew up here. Well, not here, but on the Big Island. I live in San Diego now, and I was excited about coming back, but I forgot how commercial it can feel here in Honolulu. I have a hard time with this." She motioned to the stage and the frilly decorations on the tables.

I nodded as if I agreed but knew I had no point of reference and thought I should confess that. "I haven't been to a luau before. I'm visiting from New England. My name is Hope."

"I'm Amy. Nice to meet you."

Laurie appeared just then joining in with, "And I'm Laurie. Tiki punch, anyone?"

Amy raised her eyebrows. "That depends. How drunk do you want to get?"

Fifteen

Thanks to Amy, we avoided the alcohol-saturated tiki punch, which was offered as the complimentary beverage of the luau. We sent Laurie back to the open bar for ginger ale.

Also, thanks to Amy, we had our own specialist to explain to us the tradition of the hula before the floor show began. No one else sat at our table, so we had Amy all to ourselves. She told us about how she had taken hula lessons for five years and even danced in local competitions when she was a little girl.

"You have to think of it as two separate schools of hula: ancient and modern," she said. "The ancient Hawaiians had no music. They used chants to tell the stories of old times and pass on the history of the people. The dancers never smiled. They bent their knees low to absorb the *mana* from the earth."

"The mana?" Laurie asked.

"That's the word for strength or power. You know, the spiritual energy. When the missionaries arrived, so many

Hawaiians became Christians that the ancient hula went underground."

"Why was that?" Laurie asked. "Didn't you just say it was their way of passing on history since they didn't have a written language?"

"Yes, but ancient hula—the *hula kahiko*—involved animal and human sacrifices to worship the goddess Laka. The ceremonies were performed in secret places with mysterious rituals. You can see why the missionaries had a problem with it."

Just then a young man stepped onto the stage and called out, "A-lo-ha!"

"A-lo-ha!" answered the audience.

In a far corner of the room, another young man wearing a wreath of green leaves around his head blew into a large conch shell that sounded like a deep foghorn.

"*E como mai!* Welcome!" the announcer said. Drums followed his words, and two young women in bright yellow grass skirts with tall headdresses and feathery shakers in their hands swiveled their hips at an amazing pace in time with the drums. They turned their backs to the audience and kept up in perfect rhythm. I couldn't figure out how they managed to keep the top portion of their bodies perfectly still and straight while getting so much movement going from the hips down.

The drums ended with a *tum*, and the hips froze. An unexpected *tum, tum* sounded, and the dancers' hips responded right on cue. With their hands turned knuckles in to their hips and their elbows out to the side, the two women strutted offstage.

"Do you think those were real coconut shells they were wearing on top?" Laurie whispered.

"I don't know. All I know is that I'm glad they stayed on."

"Let's give a big round of applause to our dancers, who will be coming back for your after-dinner entertainment," the announcer exclaimed.

Above the enthusiastic applause, Laurie leaned over to Amy. "I'm guessing that wasn't the ancient hula, or was it?"

"No, that was Tahitian," she said. "There's nothing Hawaiian about that. It's a crowd pleaser, as are the fire dancers."

"Is fire dancing not originally Hawaiian either?" I asked.

Amy shook her head. "Sorry to ruin all this for you."

"Are you kidding?" I said. "We'd much rather have the inside scoop. You're not ruining anything. It's the opposite. You're making this interesting for us."

"Exactly," Laurie agreed.

We were directed toward the buffet line, and again we were thankful for our personal guide. The tossed green salad and the macaroni salad were the only two items that looked familiar to me.

"What is this?" Laurie pointed to what looked like pink salsa.

"It's *lomi lomi* salmon. You should try a little of everything," Amy recommended. "I've heard they do a good job with the food here. And the *kalua* pork is actually cooked all day in an *imu*. At least that's what it says in the brochure in our rooms here at the hotel."

157

"Do I want to know what an imu is?" I asked.

"It's an underground oven. Basically it's just a hole in the ground. The whole pig is cooked all day on hot rocks and covered with *ti* leaves. The kalua pork is a typical part of an authentic luau."

I used the tongs to place some of the shredded pork on my plate. It looked good.

"And you have to try the *poi*," Amy said. "Not a lot, just enough to say you tried it."

"This is poi?" Laurie dipped her spoon into the small bowl of gray pudding. "It looks so sad. Like wallpaper paste that was left out a little too long. What does it taste like?"

"Poi," Amy said. "It grows on you after a while. You're supposed to dip your first two fingers in it and eat it that way. I mix it with the lomi lomi, and it goes down nicely."

"You don't happen to see any tortilla chips around here, do you?" Laurie asked.

Amy laughed. "Let me guess; you're from California."

"You got that right. Tortilla chips go with everything on the Left Coast, you know."

As we made our way back to the table, I wondered what my little Emilee would do with all the strange new foods I was about to send her way. To be on the safe side, I had taken one of the Hawaiian sweet dinner rolls. If nothing else, I could eat bread and salad and sip ginger ale.

I enjoyed the shredded pork more than I thought I would. I only hoped Emilee would agree when she had the opportunity to cast her vote later that night. I did cautiously try a little of everything on my plate, but only finished the pork, the salad, and the dinner rolls. Delicious.

Laurie was more adventurous and tried mixing her poi with the lomi lomi the way Amy showed her.

Amy then advised us on the square portions of *haupia* we were served for dessert. "This coconut pudding is really great. But just so you know, it can sometimes have a rather cleansing effect on your system."

"That's always a helpful bit of information," I said.

"You should hire yourself out for luaus," Laurie said. "Believe me, this would have been a less enjoyable experience if you hadn't joined us."

Amy looked appreciative of Laurie's kind words.

"I agree. I'm glad you sat with us."

"I'm glad, too," Amy said.

"You didn't finish explaining about the hula," I said. "Before the missionaries arrived, the Hawaiians didn't have a written language, and you said they didn't have music either."

"Not music as we know it today. They had drums and gourds and chants. But, yes, the Westerners brought musical instruments and songs. The Hawaiian culture changed so much in one generation. The hula came back in the form of dance that interpreted the *mele*, or you could say the poetry or the songs, that were being written about the land and the people and especially about love. The *hula 'auana*, or modern hula, interpreted those songs through more cheerful dancing."

"And that's what we think of as the hula today," Laurie surmised.

Amy nodded. "When I was taking hula lessons, we had to memorize this saying from King Kalakaua: 'Hula is the language of the heart and, therefore, the heartbeat of the Hawaiian people.'"

"That's beautiful," Laurie said.

"Did King Kalakaua happen to live during the same time as the last Hawaiian queen?" I asked.

"You mean Lili'uokalani?"

"Yes, that's the one. The one who wrote 'Aloha Oe.'"

"Oh, very good!" Amy said. "I'm impressed that you knew that. Yes, Kalakaua was her brother. He's known as the 'Merrie Monarch,' partly because he revived the hula. He also built the I'olani Palace where Lili'uokalani took over the throne after his death."

I smiled to myself. I had just found another one of Juliette's royal students. I told Amy the little bit of history I had learned about how Juliette taught these children and gave them music lessons.

"She must have had a strong influence on them," Amy said. "Because Kalakaua and Lili'uokalani helped bring a new era of music and dance to the Hawaiian culture. The first wave of missionaries tried to bury the hula; it sounds as if she helped to give new breath and life to the culture, whether she meant to or not."

"The one who came with aloha," I said.

"Yes," Amy said. "There were definitely some of those. We usually only hear about the Westerners during that era who came to capture this land and destroy the ancient arts of the Hawaiian people."

"The ones who came as haoles," I said.

"That's it," Amy agreed. "You certainly picked up a lot in only a few days."

"Thanks to people like you," Laurie said. "We have met the most amazing people here. I'm so glad we didn't go to the other luau because we wouldn't have met you, and we wouldn't have learned about the hula."

"I'm not an expert. I only know a little history and only a little hula. I can tell you this, though. Hula is something that comes out of the deep place in your heart when you listen to the poetry—the mele. You listen to the mele, and then you move in a way that gracefully interprets that truth."

I let Amy's words sink in.

God has been writing a new mele for my life. The Artist is writing a poem and stringing it together, making something beautiful and fragrant. This is His gift to me.

Before I had found a cleared place inside my soul to put such a powerful thought, the lights lowered, and the hula show began on the stage. The dancers were skilled, and their graceful motions captivated me. Even the silly and flamboyant parts of the show seemed interesting in light of Amy's earlier comments.

"You know what?" I said to Laurie the next morning, as we sat on the lanai enjoying the sparkling, clean new day. "I think the luau last night would have seemed like a Las Vegas show if Amy hadn't been with us."

"No kidding."

"Yesterday was an amazing day. The leis, the hula, the language. I love all the layers of this place."

Laurie agreed and turned her attention back to where she was reading in her new Bible. I stared out at the glistening, sapphire sea. The unfurling white waves looked freshly scrubbed after yesterday's rain. They seemed to be tumbling over each other like a litter of puppies, full of mischief.

"Listen to this," Laurie said. "It's from Matthew 11. Jesus is speaking."

"Are you tired? Worn out? Burned out on religion? Come to me. Get away with me and you'll recover your life. I'll show you how to take a real rest. Walk with me and work with me—watch how I do it. Learn the unforced rhythms of grace."

"'The unforced rhythms of grace,'" I repeated.

"Does that describe our vacation and the whole hula thing, or what?"

I tried to tell Laurie the thought I had last night about God writing a new mele for my life and how I needed to learn to move with it gracefully.

"You are moving gracefully, Hope. You're embracing this new baby and all the changes to your body with a lot of grace.

I'm the one who needs to figure out the unforced rhythms part. I'm resistant to change, especially moving."

"Are you still feeling hesitant about the house?"

"More than hesitant. But you know what? I don't want to think about that right now. I'll wait until I hear more from Gabe. Let's make some plans. You still have the tour book, right?"

"It's inside on the desk."

"Good, because I need to look up a beach I wanted to visit."

"Are you thinking we should rent a car?"

Laurie didn't answer. She had stepped inside. I thought about the two of us tootling around the island. Laurie had a thing about muscle cars and driving fast. The '68 Camaro she had driven that memorable afternoon in 1983 after she kissed Gabe in front of her parents' café was her baby. She still had the car and had paid a bundle over the years to keep it charged up in running condition.

The most exasperating phone conversations I'd had with Laurie over the past few years had been when she was roaring down her familiar wine country roads. She would put me on speakerphone, so at least I had reason to believe she was driving with both hands. However, every now and then, in the middle of a sentence, she would let out a "whoo-hooo!" and I never knew what that meant. Did she just miss hitting a jackrabbit while taking a curve at sixty miles per hour? One of these days I would work up the courage to ask her.

But not today. Today was too perfect.

"How about if we rent a car tomorrow and spend today lounging on the beach?" Laurie said, returning with the tour book and finally answering my question. "How does that sound to you?"

"Sounds great."

We didn't have to walk very far down the beach before we found a small structure that rented chairs and umbrellas. The smooth white sand felt cool on the feet. I guessed that was because the sun hadn't had a chance to thoroughly dry up the water from yesterday. We rented two beach chairs along with one blue and yellow striped umbrella and two straw mats. We were ready for anything. Both of us had stuffed our beach bags with towels, books, and sunscreen. (I had given up on the idea of a tan and had settled for moderation.) All we needed was for the rain clouds to stay far away, and we could clock out for the rest of the day.

"The weather's perfect," Laurie said. "Look at all the surfers out there. They make it look so easy."

I watched as the surfers rode the curling waves to shore, looking like action figures with posable arms bent every which way.

We watched the free show contentedly from our beach chairs, wiggling our toes in the warming sand.

"You know what this reminds me of?" Laurie asked.

"What?"

"Gidget." Laurie turned and looked at me over the top of her sunglasses. "Tell me you saw at least one of the Gidget movies."

I shook my head.

"You never saw Gidget or Moondoggie or the Big Kahuna?"

"What can I say?"

Laurie sighed. "Deborah Walley played Gidget in *Gidget Goes Hawaiian*. I don't remember who played Gidget in the first movie, but she got right out there and showed Moondoggie and the rest of them that she could surf as good as any of the boys."

Leaning back in her chair, Laurie said, "I must have watched that first movie a half dozen times when I was twelve. I wanted to be Gidget. I wanted to get up on that surfboard and show those boys that I could do it."

She laughed. "One time my mom caught me standing on top of the ironing board with my arms out, balancing back and forth."

"That's a story I never heard before."

"My mom was so mad. I left a permanent dent in the middle of her board."

"Well?" I said.

"Well, what? That's the end of the story."

"Is it really?"

"Yes, really. That's the end of my surfing story."

Lowering my sunglasses, I gave Laurie the X-ray stare she seemed to enjoy using on me. With thoughts of hula and stringing leis still floating inside, I said, "It doesn't have to be the end of your story, you know."

Sixteen

"Hope, if I were going to learn to surf like Gidget, I would have done it thirty years ago," Laurie said.

"Are you saying you think you're too old to try surfing at forty?"

"Yes."

"Then you really will be too old at fifty. And by the time you're sixty? Forget it."

Laurie scowled at me.

"Don't you see? You have to try new things while you can. You have to tell yourself you can do anything. Otherwise, you will get old. Fast. There's no reason you can't get out there and hang ten. Or at least hang on for dear life."

Laurie laughed. "That's more accurate."

"I'm serious, Laurie. Neither of us is going home from this trip regretting that we didn't do something because we were chicken. We are not chickens. We're chicks, remember? Sisterchicks. There is a difference."

Laurie kept laughing.

It took me almost half an hour, but I finally convinced her that if she passed up this opportunity, the "wish" would be there the rest of her life, but every year the "swish" would diminish a little more until it would be physically impossible.

"Okay, okay." She raised her hands in surrender. "You win."

"No, you're the one who's going to win. I'm the one who will be taking the pictures."

"My husband is never going to believe this." Laurie started to get up. Looking around she said, "If you're going to take pictures, you should be over there and turn so that you angle the shots up the beach, toward our hotel. Not toward Diamond Head."

"Okay, you know what, Little-Miss-All-Quiet-on-the-Set? Why don't you move stuff so that my chair is angled just right, and I'll go over to the beach shack to find out how to sign you up."

"Thanks, Hope. And see if they have an age limit for their insurance coverage."

I shooed away her comment and trudged through the sand wearing only my bathing suit, my dinosaur-tracking sandals, and my tangerine traumatized skin.

Oh yeah, I thought, composing a postcard for the mirror maven back home. *Check it out. Strutting along the beach at Waikiki. Turning heads. Making my monster-sized footprints on the sands of time. This Mother with a capital M is really going places now. Wish you were here! Ha!*

"Hi there," I said confidently to the white-haired youth standing beside the surf shack. "Is this where people sign up for surfing lessons?"

The beach boy looked at my belly and then tried to catch a glimpse from another angle. I guess he wanted to make sure I was really pregnant and not just hiding a beach ball under there. "We, um, like, have some restrictions."

"I'm collecting the information for my friend. The sign says you have a class every day at noon, but what can you tell me about private lessons?"

"Those are, like, more expensive."

"Oh-kay. And what else can you tell me?"

"About what?"

"About the private surfing lessons."

Did the peroxide solution he used on his hair soak through to his brain matter and bleach out a few essential cells?

"Oh, those. Yeah. Sure. You can get private lessons. From a private instructor. We have a paper here you have to sign and everything."

"Good. May I have one of those papers? My friend would like to take a private lesson. The sooner the better."

"Okay, here you go. I'll call the Big Kahuna and tell him we got a live one."

I did a good job holding in my laughter all the way back to Laurie and the beach chairs. I couldn't give away to her any of the details of my conversation. If she had just experienced what I did at the beach shack, complete with an off-site "Big Kahuna," she might have backed out. The details of my encounter could wait.

Laurie had pulled up her hair in a clip. Her mouth twitched back and forth, and she scanned the papers I handed her to sign.

"It says here they won't let pregnant women take lessons," Laurie said, looking up. "Did you see that part of the agreement? How discriminating!"

"Too bad. So sad. Oh well, it's all up to you, Gidget."

A half grin started in the corner of Laurie's face and came over her like a Honolulu sunrise. "Okay," she said resolutely. "You're right. Time to go for the wish while I still have some swish. I'm going to do this."

"Yes, you are! Get out there and show those boys how it's done." I realized I sounded like Darren when he launched into one of his coaching jags. "I'm with you all the way, Laurie. I'll be right here, taking lots of pictures."

"You better." She rose to her feet. "Because the plastic surgeon is going to want proof of how my nose got broken in so many places."

I settled comfortably in my front-row seat and made sure the camera was loaded and ready to go. Laurie had slipped on a pair of swim shorts over the bottom of her bathing suit and was standing by the surf shack, waiting for her private surf instructor to show up.

What would he look like? Would she get the bleached blond "dude" with sand permanently lodged in his brain? Or a huge, weight-lifting island boy who would hoist her onto the surfboard with the ever-popular knee in the back and arm support under the armpits? I secretly wished for the latter.

I'm happy to say I got my wish.

Laurie's Big Kahuna, her private surf instructor, was as solid as a pillar and had a great, roaring laugh that I could hear from my sheltered position under the beach umbrella.

Laurie's camera had a fantastic zoom. I could sit back and watch it all. Every so often I'd give the camera a click to capture Laurie trying out her stance on the board while it was still on the sand.

I knew Laurie would take to this sport right away. She had great balance and a skillful determination that I saw in college when she tried skateboarding for a relay event. It really was too bad she hadn't tried to surf during the two years she and I lived in Santa Barbara. We knew lots of guys at school who surfed, but I guess neither of us was exactly beach-babe material. This trip would change that stigma for Laurie.

She hoisted the sunny yellow surfboard under her arm and followed the instructor and his surfboard down to the water's edge. That's when I realized this was my chance to confiscate her film. She kept all the rolls in a zippered pouch that had a special metallic lining. I guessed the lining was to protect the film from the X-ray machines at the airport. All I had to do was snag the pouch, put it in my bag, and the deed would be done.

I put the pouch in my bag and glanced around to make sure no one had seen me take it. *That was too easy.*

Convincing myself that my thievery was for a good cause, the best cause, I returned my attention to the surfing lessons. Laurie's instructor pointed toward the water and made a rolling motion with his hands. Laurie nodded and turned to give me a lipless grin. I waved.

Timidly, Laurie approached the water. Sliding the board in front of her, she stretched out, tummy first, and daintily adjusted her legs so that her ankles were together. She started to paddle out to where her instructor was patiently floating, straddling his board as comfortably as if he were hanging out at a tailgate party. It almost looked as if he could fit a small hibachi on the end of his surfboard and cook up a few burgers while waiting for Laurie to splish-splash her way out to him.

The distance they had to paddle to reach the waves appeared to be much farther than when we were watching surfers make their way toward the shore. It looked like a lot of work.

As soon as Laurie stopped and repositioned herself on the board, I grabbed the camera again and focused in for a few shots. The instructor was right beside her on his board, showing Laurie in one fluid motion how to stand up. He lowered himself and demonstrated the procedure again. And again.

I felt nervous for Laurie because so many other surfers were out there in the same area, all vying to catch the same, slow-curling waves. I predicted a traffic jam on the more desir-able waves.

Laurie waited until the water was calm enough to try standing up. She made it on her fourth attempt and held her balance in the flat water. I shot a picture of her with her arms out like a scarecrow before she tumbled off the board. She got back on and balanced herself again, ready to stand when the next wave came.

"Look at you! You are about to surf your first wave, you clever girl, you!" I didn't care if anyone heard me; I couldn't subdue my cheerleading heart. "Way to go, Laurie!"

The instructor pointed to the rolling wave that was headed toward them. Laurie got into position and stood at just the right moment when the wave crested.

"Come on! You can do it!"

She was up!

I let out a cheer and snapped the memorable moment. Laurie was riding that wave like a pro!

In the close-up of the camera frame, I could see another surfer heading right toward her. He had what looked like a small bundle on the nose of his surfboard. Laurie leaned back slightly with her arms flapping like a marionette in slow motion. The other surfer did some sort of foot maneuver and cut his board sharply to the right just a second before he would have collided with Laurie.

The surfer went into the deep blue, but the hood ornament on his board leaped in the air and landed on the nose of

Laurie's board. She wobbled like a tightrope walker caught in an earthquake. I zoomed in the camera and couldn't believe what I saw.

It was a dog! Laurie had a confident-looking Chihuahua sitting front row on her surfboard with its ears pinned back, taking the ocean spray face first.

I started clicking shots like crazy. Awkwardly rising to my feet, I trotted down to the water and tried to focus so I could take a clear picture as Laurie came into shore. I captured a great shot of her face. Her expression was a wild mix of surprise, laughter, and pride. The dog remained stoically indifferent to the identity of its driver. He was in it for the thrill and apparently knew when to jump one ship and catch a ride with the nearest vessel heading to shore.

I waved and called out to Laurie. "You did it!" I don't know if she heard me because she was in the process of falling off into the shallow water. Her instructor was right behind her, laughing deeply. The dog was still sitting on the surfboard.

I could hear Laurie talking since they were only a few yards away. "What do I do with this little guy? Can he swim?"

"I'll take 'im. Come 'ere, Moku. He surprised you, big time, eh?"

"I didn't see where he came from."

"Dis is Moku. He's a big-time surfer like Duke Kahanamoku. He likes to take a ride any time he can get it." The instructor scooped up the wet little dog and planted him on the front of his surfboard. "You ready for another one?"

"Are you talking to me or to Moku?"

"Both."

"Sure, I'm ready." Laurie turned and waved to me. The smile on her face was a sunbeam machine, shooting out happy particles in every direction. She tossed me a big kiss and got back on her board in the forward paddle position.

"You go, Gidget!" I yelled at the top of my voice. I couldn't wait to get this roll of film developed. I clicked shots like crazy, planning to use up the roll.

Laurie caught two more waves. Neither of them brought her as close to shore or turned out as memorable as the first one. I stood and applauded, as she wearily lugged her surfboard back to the surf shack.

"Wait! One more picture," I called out. She stood in the hot sand, dripping wet, with that triumphant smile on her face and the yellow surfboard under her arm. "Look at you, surfer girl! You did it! Way to go!"

Laurie gave me a dazzling smile before tromping through the sand to return the board. Dripping and gleaming, she returned to her towel and caught her breath.

"You did it! What a little Gidget you are."

"Did you see me, Hope? I surfed!"

"I know. I got it all on film. Even the hitchhiker."

Laurie breathed out a giggle. "I couldn't believe it when that little dog jumped on the board!"

"I couldn't believe you kept your balance."

"It's much harder than it looks."

"You did great, Laurie."

"My arms are so sore."

"I noticed you went for the half-hour lesson instead of the hour."

"It was a good thing, too. I wouldn't have lasted an hour. Getting out to the waves is hard work. I'm exhausted."

"But you did it, Laurie! You went surfing. In Hawai'i. I'm so proud of you."

Laurie laughed. "Yes, I did, didn't I? Oh, wow." She drew in a deep breath, closed her eyes, and lay on her back, with her beaming face turned toward the late afternoon sun. Her smile had not yet diminished. "Thank you, Hope," she murmured on her slow float to dreamland.

"Why are you thanking me?"

"You're the one who made it happen. I wouldn't have tried surfing if you hadn't talked me into it."

"Well, thanks goes to you, too. Neither of us would be sitting here on the beach at Waikiki if you hadn't talked me into it all those years ago."

Laurie reached over to where I sat in my low beach chair and gave my ankle a squeeze. "I don't know where I'd be if it weren't for you."

"I feel the same way." I drew in the salty tang of the sea air. A fresh breeze came skittering off the waves and went to work as a tireless weaver, pulling invisible threads from my heart to Laurie's and back to mine, knitting us together, closer than ever.

"Hey, before you fall asleep," I said. "Can you tell me how to take the film out of the camera? I used up the whole roll."

Laurie leaned over, and with a few snaps, she had the film out. Then she opened her straw bag in search of a replacement roll.

"Hope, where's the pouch with the film?"

Busted.

Seventeen

I handed Laurie the pouch and watched a look of relief come over her face. My mistake had been in removing the entire pouch. I should have just removed the used film. She had so many rolls, a few wouldn't have been so easily missed. Next opportunity, I knew what to do.

As Laurie fell into a sleep of sweet contentment, I watched the surfers and thought about how I really wished I could have tried surfing with Laurie. My husband and sons would have been so proud of me. I would have been proud of me.

Oh, well, little Emilee and I would have to find something else that the two of us could do that didn't require extra insurance coverage. Perhaps the contentment season I was entering meant I should be satisfied with sitting back and watching my "older" friend while she did all the swimming with the dolphins. Or at least with the Chihuahuas.

I reached into my bag for the book about Juliette Cooke

that I'd bought at the Mission Houses Museum. At least I could comfort myself with some soothing history of the Victorian era. I flipped open to one of Juliette's journal entries near the back.

November 30, 1855

I thought my duties in peopling the earth were over, having lived to the age of 43 and been the mother of 6 human beings, but it seems likely to be otherwise. According to present appearances, the month of March may see me again a mother.

I grinned. Not only did this woman serve tea to Hawaiian royalty and teach their children to read and write music, but also, just like me, she had another baby later in life.

A following journal entry caught my eye because the word *Waikiki* was listed next to the date. I wondered how different this beach I was sitting on had been when Juliette made the entry on October 10, 1860.

Waikiki…has become the fashionable bathing place of the foreigners… The tide comes in, and we all, even to little Clarence, rig in our bathing dresses and hats and sally forth… The girls all swim…a great squealing and laughing…ducking them, head and all under water—sometimes hauling them out to sea.

I read a bit more and learned that Juliette's baby had been a ten-pounder. Then I leaned back, letting the information sink in. Juliette had bobbed in the waves on this very same beach almost 150 years ago. She apparently didn't let life happen to everyone else while she sat back and watched.

That's when I realized I couldn't wait another minute. If that New England missionary woman could have a baby at the age of forty-four and go swimming in the Pacific at the age of forty-eight, what was I doing sitting in this beach chair? I was only thirty-nine!

With a strong-armed push, I stood, flipped off my sunglasses, kicked off my sandals, and set my face toward the deep blue sea. "Laurie?"

"Yes?"

"I'm going in the water."

"Okay, have fun," she murmured.

"I will."

With my chin high, I sallied forth into the ageless Pacific. I didn't stall or take the water inch-by-inch to acclimate myself. I stepped right into the shimmering blue until it was up to my thighs, and then I dove under.

Oh, the sensation of coming up, covered in glittering drops of warm salt water with all the tiny liquid diamonds forming rainbows on my eyelashes. Being careful to find an area where the surfers weren't charging toward the shore, I hauled my little Emilee out to sea, where we kicked and floated and splashed around with abandon. Several times I heard myself laughing aloud.

What was that verse in Psalm 100? Something about "bring a gift of laughter." That's what I'm bringing to You today, Lord, because You have filled me with such joy!

The shore looked different from this vantage point in the water, not the same as when we were in the catamaran. I felt like a mermaid, popping my head up to see the stretch of white sand dotted with people. Beyond the sand was a gathering of trees at Kapiolani Park. Rising behind the trees, *mauka*, were the hills that lined a broad, green valley. I floated on my back, watching a flock of fluffy clouds hop over the hills like spring lambs out for a frolic while the trade winds tried to herd them back out to sea.

In all the world there can't be a more beautiful place than right here, right now.

Slowly puttering my way toward shore on the tail of a frothy wave, I rose and shook the salt water from my ears and hair. I could feel Emilee doing itty-bitty flip-flops as I strode back to my towel.

"Hey, little surfer girl," Laurie greeted me and handed me a towel to dry my face. "I saw you out there splashing around. Looked like you were having fun."

"It was delicious! This is the most beautiful place I've ever been. The water is so warm."

"I know. Hey, don't lie down yet. I fixed your spot. Now you can lie on your stomach. I hollowed out a little dip so Emilee can burrow in the sand."

"You're too good to me, Laurie."

"I try."

After slathering myself with more sunscreen, I nestled in my custom-designed space and kept telling Laurie how beautiful the water was.

"You know," she said. "I think God must really enjoy the way you appreciate His creation so much."

"Why do you say that?"

"Even in college you were always noticing the moon or the shape of a certain leaf. You appreciate the beauty of creation more than anyone I know. I thought of that the other evening when you read that verse about inviting God to enjoy His creation."

"Oh, right. In Psalm 104."

"I've been thinking about that, because I know what it's like to enjoy something I've created."

"Like your photos," I said.

"Exactly. But what would it be like for the thing that was created to turn around and express mutual enjoyment of the moment to the Creator?"

I wasn't sure I followed her.

"Think of all the criticism God must hear every day. But not from you, Hope. Every day I hear you express awe and delight for everything around you that He created. You are enjoying His work of art right alongside Him, yet you are part of that work of art. Can you imagine how that must make Him feel?"

I couldn't.

"I think I understand something I never understood before."

"What's that?" The revelations seemed to be coming at Laurie so quickly I couldn't even try to keep up.

"I think I understand how deeply the Creator must love the parts of His creation that love Him back."

"Laurie, you definitely are getting wise in your old age."

She didn't respond. She seemed deep in thought.

I closed my eyes and settled in for a little snooze. I slept so soundly that when I woke, I told Laurie she should patent her sand-belly bed and find a way to sell it to pregnant women who had a hard time getting comfortable enough to fall asleep.

"The sand might get a little messy," she said. "But aside from that, sure. Why not?"

"What was that Hawaiian oven Amy told us about last night?"

"The imu?"

"Yes. You could call your invention the imu and sell it to people on the islands who have beach houses because they're used to a lot of sand everywhere, right?"

"Hope, they use an imu to roast little piggies."

"Oh, that's right. Never mind."

Deciding we were done roasting our thoroughly salted little piggies in the hot sand, Laurie and I returned our beach equipment to the "dude" at the surf shack and headed back to our room. But we got sidetracked when we saw the Saturday market at Kapiolani Park across the street from the beach.

From a distance, it appeared similar to flea markets I'd frequented in Connecticut, with two notable differences. First, the ever-present trade winds kept the tarp flaps in motion. It looked like the blue sheets were cooling themselves and their shelterees with languid fanning motions. That did not happen at New England flea markets. The summer air sits upon my corner of the world like a fat and sassy cat who only occasionally flicks its tail to give the impression of some movement. I much preferred the island breezes.

The second difference was the types of items sold. Aside from the usual T-shirts, candles, and handmade silver jewelry, this outdoor market carried things I'd never seen sold at home. One booth offered wind chimes made of coconut shells. Another carried polished gourds and teakwood salad bowls. We passed a booth that sold lava stones and shark teeth. These two items were wrapped with braided twine, and a sign promised increased energy flow to the *kapu* regions of the brain when worn around the forehead.

Laurie and I kept walking.

The booth that caught our attention was one where an artist sat doing calligraphy. His gray-streaked hair swirled down his back in one long tendril, like a tornado. He appeared to be in his fifties, but his skin looked as though it was already in its eighties.

Hanging from a Peg-Board behind him were dozens of names written in rainbow-colored calligraphy. All the names were in Hawaiian. A list hung nearby showing the English and Hawaiian versions of names.

"There's your name," Laurie said.

Hope was "Mana'olana," Laurie was "Lali," Emilee Rose was "Emele? Loke," and Darren was "Kaleni."

"I wonder if all my girls are listed." Laurie scanned the list.

"Any name you want in calligraphy, I can do it," the artist said. "English, Japanese, Hawaiian…doesn't matter."

Laurie wrote down her daughters' names, and he went to work on the three masterpieces.

I didn't bother to have him write out my sons' names in Hawaiian, English, or Japanese because I knew they weren't likely to be impressed with such a souvenir.

The artist worked swiftly and skillfully. He spoke each of the names aloud before touching the brush to the paper.

"I love the way the Hawaiian language sounds," I said to Laurie. "I wish we had asked Kapuna Kalala to teach us more Hawaiian words when we were making the leis."

"Kapuna Kalala?" The artist looked up from his work. "She is highly honored in this area. There aren't many *kapunas* left."

"Isn't *Kapuna* her first name?" I asked.

"No, it's a title. A kapuna is a wise, elderly Hawaiian woman of distinction."

"Well, she certainly is all of that," Laurie said.

"Did the kapuna come near to you when she was teaching you?" he asked.

"She got very close to Hope when we were about to leave," Laurie said. "She said a prayer over Hope and Emilee Rose."

He dipped his head toward my middle. "Emilee Rose?"

I nodded, touching my tummy. "I'd like you to make a

name sign for Emilee, when you've finished with the ones for Laurie's girls."

Undeterred from his previous question, in spite of a new order, he asked again, "Did she come near to you? Did she breathe on you?"

"Yes. When she hugged me and said aloha, it was like she was breathing over me."

He nodded the sort of slow head bob that comes when a person is contemplating a deep truth before speaking.

We waited to hear what he had to say.

Eighteen

"Do you know the meaning of the word *aloha?*" the artist asked Laurie and me. The trade winds rippled across the blue tarp that covered his humble art studio.

"Doesn't it mean, 'hello,' 'good-bye,' or 'love'?" Laurie asked.

He nodded. "But do you know where the word comes from?"

"No."

I was curious but at the same time slightly on guard for clever, flea-market tactics. I was prepared to turn down anything he tried to sell us beyond the few pieces we had ordered. But he seemed more bent on imparting knowledge to us than making another buck.

"*Alo* means 'presence' or literally, 'in the face.' *Ha* means 'breath' or 'spirit.' So, *aloha* means 'to breathe into the face or share spirit with another.'"

"Hope, that's what you've been saying it feels like when the island breezes come rushing at us—like the wind is breathing over us."

"People who share aloha are those who draw close to another," the artist said. "They come close enough to trust another with the essence of who they are, close enough to breathe in your face. That's why I asked if Kapuna Kalala breathed on you." A slow grin elevated the wrinkles in his face. "She gave you her aloha."

"That's quite a bit more than hello, good-bye, or I love you," Laurie said quietly.

"Although, in some ways, it seems to include all of that at once," I said.

The artist tapped his forehead. "The ancient Hawaiians used to go forehead to forehead when they greeted each other. Some of my Hawaiian friends who live on Molokai greet me that way when I see them."

Laurie and I looked at each other hesitantly. I hoped she didn't feel the compunction to try out this technique, because it had been a long time since I'd brushed my teeth that morning.

She suppressed a chuckle. "You would have to be pretty comfortable with a person before you could go forehead to forehead when you greeted them."

"That's right," he said, returning to his craft. "I have read that King Kamehameha the Great, on his deathbed, went forehead to forehead with George Vancouver and breathed his aloha on him."

"Who was Vancouver?" Laurie asked.

"An explorer who originally sailed with Captain Cook when they stumbled on these islands in the late 1700s. Cook was killed on the Big Island, you know. Vancouver returned three times. Not all the Caucasians who came here were haoles."

"Haole," I repeated. "No breath."

He looked up, surprised. "That's right. With aloha, you can trust your spirit or breath to another. With a haole, there is no breath."

I started to cry. I could say it was hormones that pushed the big, globby tears to the surface, but I think it was something else. Something deeper and truer.

Laurie patted my arm tenderly. "You okay?"

I nodded and stepped away from the booth, sopping up the tears with the edge of my beach towel.

When I returned, I asked Laurie, "Doesn't it seem like you've heard this before? Like the faint memory of a story or a dream?"

"Which part?" she asked.

"The breathing on someone part. The aloha. It's such a beautiful image, but I can't quite figure out why it seems so familiar."

As I tried to put my memories and tear ducts back in working order, Laurie paid for the art, praising the artist warmly. I bought Emilee's name in calligraphy, and Laurie bought two of the premade framed pictures of the word *aloha* calligraphied in shades of deep ocean blue.

"Our souvenirs," she said. "So we can remember this."

I didn't think I'd need calligraphy to remind me of anything about this trip. Especially the word *aloha*. But I appreciated Laurie's kindness and told her so.

As we strolled through the park, many of the vendors were taking down their stalls and calling it a day.

"Did I ever tell you that my mom came here in the fifties?" Laurie asked. "Her parents brought the family here for vacation soon after Hawai'i became a state. She said it was a pity because you and I wouldn't find any of the 'old' Hawai'i left. I think she's wrong. I think it's extraordinary the way we've been exposed to such a blending of the old and the new."

"I know. I wonder if most tourists have similar experiences, or if God is doing something for the two of us."

"Like what?"

"I'm not sure. But the whole 'unforced rhythm of grace' concept with the hula and the kapuna with the leis, and now the meaning of *aloha*..."

"I think all of it is to prepare you to be a graceful, loving mama this second time around."

I was surprised that Laurie thought all the lessons applied to me. "I was thinking it was all about you doing something with your art. I mean, think of that man back there with his calligraphy. What a unique talent. Yet he's using it. And I'm glad he is."

Laurie stopped in front of a tie-dyed T-shirt booth and wagged her finger at me. "No, you don't. Stop right there. It's one thing for you to talk me into getting up on a surfboard, but I'm not ready to start selling my art at a flea market."

"Who said anything about flea markets?"

"You did."

"I was only trying to say that…never mind." I had the same feeling inside that I get when I'm at church and the pastor is preaching an especially convicting sermon. I tend to look around and think of how the other people in the pews really should be paying attention to his words.

"Go ahead. What were you trying to say?" Laurie's expression softened.

"I shouldn't be projecting all this on you. All I'm saying is that your photos are wonderful. You should do something with them."

"So you've said."

"And so I'll probably keep on saying, so prepare yourself."

Laurie linked her arm in mine, and as we started walking, she said, "Thanks for the warning."

I was more determined than ever to snatch the rolls of film from Laurie's bag and find a place that would develop them quickly. If we could look at them together, she would see the difference between the photos I took and the ones she took. She would see that she needed to pursue this talent.

I eyed her bag, swinging over her other shoulder. While she was in the shower, I'd remove the film and put it in my purse. Then first chance I had, I would find a place to have them developed.

Meanwhile, we amiably settled into a relaxing afternoon and evening that included simultaneous cell phone conversations with our husbands while we strolled along the beach walkway on Kalakaua Avenue. Then we took in two fun movies on the hotel television and an entire box of chocolate-covered macadamia nuts.

I forgot about the photos until we were about to go to bed. Laurie was on the phone, reserving a rental car for us and pulled out the film pouch while digging for her wallet. I hoped she would leave the pouch on the desk, but she was too organized. With Laurie, everything had a place, and the pouch went back into its designated corner of the straw bag.

Tomorrow. In the morning. While she's in the bathroom.

But again, I forgot. Instead, we concentrated on packing up everything we thought we would need for a full day away from the hotel. We had arranged to have the rental car delivered to us at the hotel so we could go directly to the morning service at the coral-block Kawaiaha'o Church, across the street from the Mission Houses Museum.

The elevator had just deposited us in the lobby when Laurie said, "Did you grab the tour book?"

I checked my bulging bag. "No, it must still be on the desk."

"I'll get it." Laurie fumbled for her room key.

"Leave all your stuff here," I suggested.

She left with only the room key, and I suddenly realized I had all the film. This was my chance, and I had to take it quickly.

"Excuse me," I asked the concierge, lugging our gear over to the desk. "Can you tell me how I can get some film developed quickly?"

"The corner market has a one-hour developing service. Would you like us to take it there for you?"

I remembered how selective Laurie was about where she took her film at home.

"Do you know of any professional film services on the island that could develop it in a day or two?"

"Yes, we have several we work with regularly. We can help you with that."

"Good. Then let me leave this film with you. I need to get it back by Tuesday, and the price doesn't matter. All that matters is that you take it to the company that will do the best job."

I handed over the rolls of film and felt like a terrible sneak as I filled out the paperwork for the concierge.

Laurie returned with the guidebook, and we took off in our rental car, rolling along at a nice, respectful pace through town. I wondered how long she would be able to drive so sedately. You see, she had rented a convertible. A red Mustang convertible.

The darling was just screaming to be let loose.

However, the streets of Waikiki didn't provide such an opportunity. And the streets of neighboring Honolulu around the Kawaiaha'o Church didn't offer a lot of parking.

"I can let you out here," Laurie suggested. We were stopped behind another car on a narrow road that divided the Mission Houses Museum and the back side of the church. "I'll find a parking spot and then meet you inside."

"Okay." I started to climb out of the car, but my lei got caught on the headrest. It wasn't the lei Laurie had made for me but rather the purple orchid birthday lei she had bought me the first night at the gift shop. The flowers had stayed fresh in our room refrigerator, and I wanted to wear the lei to church this morning. Laurie had hung hers over a lamp shade in our room because she wanted to dry it out before taking it home.

Untangling my lei from the headrest, I gave Laurie a wave and stepped into the beautiful garden area behind the large church. To my left was a wrought iron gate that opened to a cemetery. Two aged plumeria trees towered on either side of the gate. I stopped to look at the trees. They held no fragrant white blossoms on this January morning, yet I still had to stare at their beauty.

Obviously they had been planted here long ago. Every one of their many slender, curved branches seemed to reach heavenward with an air of graceful elegance. I tried to imagine the magnificent canopy these trees made when they were in full bloom. I stood amazed at how two simple trees could perform such an act of silent praise by just *being*.

Since we were early for the service, I wandered into the small graveyard. My eye caught on a short, block-shaped gravestone a few feet away. Across the top, in raised letters, was the word *MOTHER*. Taking a few steps closer to the gravestone, I ran my fingers across the raised letters carved into the thick, white marble block. It reminded me of last week when I had my hormone meltdown and how I told Darren I was a Mother with a capital *M*. Whoever was buried in this grave was apparently a mother with *all capital letters.*

I bent to read the name on the front of the simple grave marker.

JULIETTE M. COOKE

MAR. 12, 1812

AUG. 11, 1896

Precious in the sight of the Lord

Is the death of His saints.

"Juliette," I whispered. "My little missionary woman!"

I stepped back and started to cry. I'd never cried at a cemetery. Especially not in front of a grave of someone I'd never met.

But then, I felt as if I had met Juliette. I'd visited her house. I'd stood in her kitchen and heard about how she used forty eggs to make nice tea cakes for the Hawaiian kings. I'd turned into a bobbing Bettie in the same ocean into which she had "sallied forth" more than a 150 years earlier.

And here she was, marked for all time as a mother with capital M-O-T-H-E-R.

The tall grave marker to the left of Juliette's was that of her husband, Amos, who had passed away twenty-five years before her. That meant Juliette spent a quarter of a century as a widow. Instead of returning to New England, she had stayed here on Oahu.

This really was your home, wasn't it? These were your people. You lived your life, all the blissful parts and all the painful parts, on this island.

Gathering my composure, I touched the word MOTHER again, and then, with one gliding motion, I lifted the purple orchid lei from around my neck and placed it lovingly across the marble grave marker.

"A garland of hosannas," I whispered. "Wear it well, dear Juliette. I give it to you with my aloha."

Remembering the description of aloha that the artist at the flea market had explained, I smiled and thought, *I can't exactly go forehead to forehead and breathe out my aloha on you now, Juliette. Maybe in heaven. Watch for me, okay? I don't suppose there will be any tea parties I can help you prepare, but maybe you and I can sally forth to the shore along the river of life. You bring your little Clarence, and I'll bring my Emilee Rose.*

I realized I was conjuring up a dream that was outside my short life. I was dreaming about eternity. If anyone had heard me, they would surely have thought I was crazy to be standing here, making plans with a dead woman.

But if all God's promises were true, and I wholeheartedly believed they were, then there was nothing crazy about dreaming of heaven. I had every reason to believe that, just as God had written my name in His Book of Life, He would take me into His home when I left this earth. And what endless possibilities awaited His children in His house. The stories have not yet been told. The leis have not yet been strung.

Filled, filled, filled with tingles of wonder, I stepped softly across the green tufts of thick tropical grass and closed the gate, leaving the sacred graveyard. Now I knew why the two plumeria trees guarding the gate couldn't help but lift their slender branches upward, toward the heavens.

Taking the coral steps up to the front of the church, I watched for Laurie but didn't see her. Inside the large sanctuary were dozens of long, straight-backed pews made of a rich, shiny, dark wood. I guessed it was the same koa wood used in the small mirror I'd bought at the Mission Houses gift shop. The contrast of the nearly black wood against the simple, whitewashed coral-block walls was striking, especially with the arched, deep-set glass windows. This was a hallowed meeting place filled with much love.

Aloha nui loa. Isn't that what the kapuna said? Much love.

It struck me that the aloha, the breath, was literal here, in that the cool air flowed freely through the slatted windows and prepared the sanctuary for worship by bringing the first fruit of fragrance to the altar.

I was invited to take a seat and made my way halfway to the front and sat on the left side, in about the same area our family sat in our church at home. Settling in quietly and feeling the breeze across my neck, I kept watching for Laurie and wondered where Juliette used to sit when she came to services here. Did her family have a select row, the way many New England churches had plaques embedded in their pews for the established families in the community?

I noticed the mix of parishioners seated around me. It seemed as if nearly every ethnic group was represented. Most of the older women were dressed in flowing mu'umu'us. They greeted each other warmly with kisses on the cheek.

The service began with a prayer in Hawaiian. My head was bowed, but my ears were standing at full attention so as not to miss a single syllable.

I checked again for Laurie and rose with the rest of the congregation to sing the first hymn. I was thrilled to see that the words were in Hawaiian. Even though I'm not much of a singer, I opened my mouth wide, as if I could somehow catch the words and music flowing around me and persuade them to go inside.

Laurie quietly slipped in beside me on the last stanza and held the hymnbook with me. We were seated while the announcements were made and the offering collected. Laurie had been flipping through the hymnal and tapped me, pointing to a small paragraph printed at the bottom of page 159:

I remember one public examination of the Young Chiefs' School held in Kawaiaha'o Church, crowded with interested spectators and friends, which was of superior excellence. The singing was led by Mrs. Cooke [Juliette Montague], who had no instrument and raised the pitch by her tuning fork. She had a voice of singular power and clearness that soared above all others in our assemblages.
—Martha A. Chamberlain

"Isn't this Juliette the one you've been talking about?"

I nodded.

The congregation stood again for the next hymn, Beethoven's "Joyful, Joyful, We Adore Thee." I sang my little heart out, half listening for Juliette's voice of "singular power and clearness" to soar above all the others.

When we reached the third verse with the words, "Flowery meadow, flashing sea, chanting bird and flowing fountain, call us to rejoice in Thee," everything within me yearned to raise my lanky limbs like the plumeria trees and offer my meager praise all the way up to heaven.

However, once again, my conservative upbringing and New England nurturing held fast. I stood staunch, barely moving, despite the holiness of the moment. I felt caught in a struggle over wanting to be one who moved with grace—with aloha—and yet finding myself stuck in a self-conscious bog. *Haole. No breath. I have much to learn about living the unforced rhythm of grace.*

When the service ended, Laurie said, "What happened to your lei?"

I told Laurie about the graveyard and how I found Juliette's grave marker and left my lei there.

"I brought my camera with me," Laurie said. "We could take some pictures, if that doesn't sound too strange."

I was all for it but hoped we weren't overstepping our boundaries or appearing too much like tourists.

No one was around when Laurie snapped pictures at the

gate into the graveyard. I was glad she was taking some shots of the plumeria trees.

"Gabe would love this place," she murmured. "It's such a peaceful hideaway."

I stood beside Juliette's grave marker, my hand resting on the lei as Laurie moved around looking for the best angle. She took several shots, and I told her I definitely wanted copies. Then I felt convicted.

"Laurie, I have a confession to make."

She lowered the camera and looked at me, surprised, as if I should have done all my confessing while I was inside the church.

"I sent your film out to be developed because I didn't want to have to wait until we got home to see all the pictures."

"Where did you send it?" The look on her face was not one I had hoped to ever see again. It was the same look she gave me our freshman year, when I confessed that I'd tossed her white silk blouse into the wash with my undies and a stray red sock. She forgave me admirably that time because it was a genuine accident. This time it was premeditated.

"I asked the concierge to send it to a reliable place."

"A reliable place?"

"A professional film developing service."

Laurie pulled out her cell phone and tapped in some numbers. "Why didn't you ask me?" She still looked relatively calm.

"It was supposed to be a surprise. But I didn't think it

through all the way. I should have talked with you about it. It is your film."

"Hello, I'd like the concierge, please."

I walked over to a bench by the front gate and sat down while Laurie asked about her film.

"It all started with that rainbow coming out of her nose," I muttered with a sigh.

Laurie walked toward me while she listened to the concierge. She appeared satisfied with the information she was getting and said, "Thanks" before closing her phone.

"Sorry," I said.

"It's okay. Come on. I'm parked a couple of blocks away."

We walked in silence. Just as we got to the car, Laurie said, "This reminds me of what happened our second semester, when I sold back your literature textbook two days before you took your final. I was trying to get a running start."

"I'd forgotten about that."

"Are we even now?"

"I wasn't trying to get even!" I climbed in the car, and we flipped a couple of levers, pushed a button, and the top of our car slowly retracted.

"I know. I'm just trying to say don't worry about it, Hope. It should be fine. It'll be fun to have the pictures to look at together. They won't be done until Tuesday. Now I have something to ask you." She flipped on her sunglasses and handed me a map of the island. "Would you mind if we drove out to Waimanalo Beach? It's by the blowhole at Halona."

"Never heard of either of them, but it's fine with me."

"The tour book said that Waimanalo is the beach where *From Here to Eternity* was filmed."

"Ah. Why didn't I know that?"

Laurie grinned at my sarcasm. "You mind being the navigator? The beach is right about here." She pointed to a spot on the map.

I leaned back, studying what route we should take, while she pulled our red-hot set of wheels away from the curb.

"I wanted to find the beach where they filmed the nurses' scene in *South Pacific*," Laurie said. "But that beach is on a different island. Kauai, I think."

"'Gonna wash that man right outa my hair,'" I responded.

"Hey, I'm impressed! A classic movie that you know. A musical, even."

"Don't be impressed. My high school did *South Pacific* my senior year, and I was the class treasurer so I ended up at a lot of the performances selling tickets."

"Do you remember this one?" Laurie launched into one of the songs from *South Pacific*. I knew all the lyrics and sang along with her. We were having a grand time of it until we stopped at a red light. With the top down, there was no hiding that we were a couple of middle-aged tourists in an obnoxiously red convertible, singing a selection of Broadway hits at the top of our lungs.

Laurie reached over and pretended to turn off the radio, as if all the singing had been coming from a random sound wave that hit a freakish sunspot and ended up on our FM, easy-listening station.

The light turned green, and we exchanged chuckle-smirks.

"Which way?" Laurie asked.

"You need to get in the left lane so you can turn left at this next street."

"I can't. The next street is one way."

"You're kidding." I looked at the map and at the name of the street we were on.

"I'm turning right," Laurie said.

"Okay, but then turn left as soon as you can."

We drove in circles for several minutes before Laurie spotted the on-ramp for H-1. "Is this it?"

"Yes, get in the right lane. Quick."

Laurie whipped over into the right lane and with a heavy foot on the gas, we roared onto the freeway. Or maybe I should say, we roared onto the parking lot.

"Where are all these people going?" Laurie spouted.

"The beach?"

"This is worse than traffic in San Francisco." She turned on the radio. No freakish, sunspot-induced musicals belted out. Only the mellow twang of a slack key guitar playing a lulling, tropical tune.

"I need something a little more lively." Laurie punched a button and evoked a pounding, rhythmic number, complete with vulgarities. We both quickly pushed the next button and listened to the surf report for the North Shore, as if we actually understood all the terms used to describe the conditions.

"I don't want to move," Laurie said all of a sudden.

"We aren't moving." I pointed to the traffic ahead of us. "At least we're not moving very fast."

"No, I mean I don't want to move to San Francisco. We'd be in traffic like this all the time. I don't want to start all over again. I don't care if the house is a great price or the entry has Italian marble or even if it had a dozen bathrooms. I don't want a different house."

"Have you told Gabe any of this?"

"No. I hadn't even told myself until this minute."

"You should tell him."

She held both arms out straight in a rigid ten and two position on the steering wheel. "I don't want to tell him." Then she tossed me a playful look. "You tell him."

"I'm not going to tell him. He's your husband. Why don't you want to tell him?"

"Because…"

I waited for more words to tumble out of her heart.

The traffic began to open up. It appeared that a lot of the motorists were getting off on the exit that led to Waikiki Beach. Perhaps we would have clear sailing as soon as we got out of the touristy pocket of town.

"I don't want to tell Gabe because what if this is his big dream, and I snatch it away from him? What if he listens to me, and we stay where we are but both regret it later? What if I really regret it because every time I think of what we could have had if we moved, I'll know we didn't take the leap because of me?"

"It's a huge decision," I said.

"It is."

"It's a mutual decision. For all you know, Gabe might be thinking these same things, but he hasn't had a chance to tell you."

"Doubtful." Laurie picked up a little speed and switched to the fast lane. "I wish all this could have waited until next week. I'm trying to be on vacation here."

She passed the car in front of us with a quick lane-change maneuver that I never would have attempted due to the minimum amount of space. We bobbed smoothly back into the fast lane and she spouted, "You know, actually, if I allowed myself to be perfectly honest, I would have to say that I'm pretty angry about the timing on this."

I was all for honesty but dearly wished Laurie had made her confession back at the church. Or at least at the graveyard, like I had. The only thing that was keeping her from coaxing our little Mustang past forty miles per hour was the congestion on the road.

"Laurie," I said, using my best soothing voice. "You know what? You don't have to decide about the house today. You haven't signed anything. There's plenty of time to call Gabe and talk it through with him. Just pretend you really are on vacation."

Her arms relaxed. "You're right. And I don't have to pretend. I am on vacation. We're in Hawai'i."

"Yes, we are."

Laurie paused a moment and then turned on the radio again. She pushed the first button and returned to the station with the palm-tree-swaying island melodies. Raising the volume, she leaned back and with a drippy Southern accent said, "For the remainder of our vacation, Miss Laurinda Sue will be playing the role of Scarlett O'Hara on the nurses' beach in Hawai'i."

"I have no idea what that means, but if it's some sort of anger management technique, I'm all for it."

She started to sing her own words to the lulling tropical tune on the radio. "I'm going to wash that man right out of my hair because after all, tomorrow is another day."

Nineteen

The dark lava rocks that formed the tall encasement around the Waimanalo Beach appeared treacherous as Laurie and I stood on the edge looking over the side at the famous "Eternity Beach."

"It looked so different in the movie," Laurie said wistfully. "So majestic."

"I imagine it is more majestic when you're down there on the beach, tucked in by those protective cliffs."

"How did they ever get the film crew down there fifty years ago? The lighting would have been tricky, don't you think? And the sound would have been a challenge, too, because of the echo of the waves."

I studied Laurie. "You are just a little cinema-head, aren't you?"

"Why do you say that?" Laurie looked at me over the top of her sunglasses.

"Who else would come to a place like this and evaluate lighting and sound?"

"I guess you're right. So? Do you want to chance it, or should we drive on?"

"Why don't you go on down," I said, motioning to the *From Here to Eternity* beach. "I'll wait in the car. I wanted to have another look at the tour book, so take your time."

Laurie tossed me the car keys and reached into the open car for her camera. "I won't be long."

I made myself busy organizing the stuff in the trunk and covering my exposed skin with sunscreen. The sun felt intense. We had raided our little refrigerator in the hotel room and brought several bottles of water and juice with us. They were ice cold when we had stuck them in the trunk that morning. Now they were so hot I could have managed to make a respectable cup of tea out of one of them.

Fortunately, Laurie wasn't gone long, so I didn't get fried while sitting in the car reading through the tour book and snacking on a bag of trail mix.

"It was much more appealing in the movie," she said. "I mean, it's a nice little spot, but those film guys definitely found just the right angle."

I offered her a bottle of warm water, and we were back on the narrow highway, heading around the perimeter of Oahu.

"The tour book says that one of the beaches we passed a little ways back is good for snorkeling. Are you interested?" I asked.

"Sure. That sounds fun. They probably have a place to rent masks and snorkels, right?"

"Yep. And they even have public rest rooms."

Laurie flashed me a wry grin. "Then we definitely should stop, right?"

I nodded. "One bottle of water, and I'm a goner."

The parking was a challenge on this busy Sunday afternoon, as was the hike down to the ocean. We were rewarded with pristine waters, a sandy beach, and a grove of graceful palm trees—every amenity the tour book had promised. Laurie and I found the rest rooms and changed into our bathing suits.

Clambering toward the water with all our gear, we agreed on a nice, open spot in the hot sand and settled in like two birds feathering their spring nest. Laurie got a call from Gabe, so I moseyed over to the rental shack to see about acquiring two masks and snorkels.

"Ready?" I asked Laurie, holding up the masks and snorkels.

"Ready for what?"

"Ready to jump in the water and spy on the fish."

By the scowl on Laurie's face, I could tell she already had jumped. But it was into a deep blue funk instead of the deep blue sea.

"You've been thinking about the move, haven't you?"

"How could you tell?"

"Your Southern accent is gone. I'm guessing you're not

playing the role of Scarlett anymore."

"Not when I get a call like that."

"What did Gabe say?"

"He's really excited about the house. He's already asked an architect friend of ours to draw up plans for a new studio."

"Did you tell him how you're feeling about the move?"

"I mostly listened to him, but then I told him some of the reasons I'm hesitant."

"What did he say?"

"He said a lot of things, including how he would walk away from the whole deal if I don't have peace about it."

"I knew I always liked that guy."

"But Hope, don't you see the pressure that puts on me? It's all up to me to make the decision now. As far as he's concerned, it's all green lights."

I pulled a bottle of extremely warm water from my beach bag and sipped it slowly, contemplating Laurie's dilemma.

"You know what I think?" I said after a minute.

"What?"

"I think you should put on this mask and snorkel and go out there and soak your head."

Laurie didn't laugh the way I'd hoped she would.

"I'm serious, Laurie. Go for a swim. Wash this stuff right outa your hair. Get your mind off it. Pray about it. Relax. Enjoy the day."

"Go soak my head, huh?"

"I meant that in the nicest, sweetest way, you understand."

"Of course." I saw the hint of a grin as she reached for the mask and snorkel.

Turning to an older couple settled on the beach a few feet from our towels, I said, "Would you mind keeping an eye on our stuff while we're in the water?"

"Sure. No worries. You can bring us back some sushi."

"That sounds like a great idea for dinner," Laurie said.

I gave her a long glare to see if she was joking. She wasn't.

"What? You're not a sushi fan yet?"

"No."

"Well, now I have a challenge before me."

"No you don't," I said. "I'm not going to try sushi on this trip."

"*Try* sushi? You mean you've never tried it?"

We were at the water now, ankle deep, swishing out our masks and adjusting the straps.

"No, I have never tried sushi, and I think it would be just fine with me if I never did." Then, to further make my point, I added, "On such a perfect afternoon as this, when we are about to pay a friendly visit to the fish in this bay, I'd prefer we didn't talk about eating them. Raw."

"Hope?"

"What?"

"Go soak your head." Laurie grinned. "I mean that in the sweetest way possible, of course."

"Of course."

What I didn't expect when I eased into the warm water

and soaked my head was that I was about to be introduced to an entire world of spectacular fish. The variety, shapes, and colors astounded me. Dozens and dozens of amazing little creatures darted about the coral, seemingly unbothered by our intrusion in their watery ecosystem.

Laurie tapped me on the leg. We surfaced and removed our snorkels.

"This is amazing!" she said. "Did you see those bright yellow ones with the tall fin and the black stripes?"

"They're beautiful! All I can hope is that they didn't hear you talking about you-know-what before we got in the water."

Laurie laughed, and we went back under.

The gentle rhythm of the tide in this large lagoon rocked me as I easily floated along. I was captured, drawn into this liquid fairyland where fronds of green seaweed rose in forestlike clumps and swayed back and forth to music my mortal ear couldn't hear.

In and out of the dancing forest, the eager fish swam. My favorites were the schools of iridescent silver and blue fish that were about the size of a large safety pin, only more narrow and sleek. They zipped to and fro as a group. Each time they banked to the right or left, my eye caught a glimmer of the luminous rainbow colors hidden in their silvery scales.

A young girl came up beside us in our gigantic aquarium and released a handful of green peas into the water. From every direction the fish came toward her, gobbling the peas in one bite.

I let out a squeal through the snorkel. The girl released another handful, and the fish rushed toward her again.

"Did you see that?" I asked, as Laurie and I simultaneously surfaced.

She said something unintelligible because she hadn't taken the snorkel out of her mouth. She laughed, took it out, and repeated, "Feeding frenzy! Did you see how they came from all directions? And for green peas, too. My kids never came running for peas."

"You didn't have boys," I said. "All I have to do is say *food*, and they come storming in, just like those fish."

"Do you miss them?" Laurie asked, as we treaded water.

"A little."

"I miss mine a little, too."

We looked at each other, looked at the shore where the elderly couple sat watching our gear, and looked at the water as if we had choreographed the move.

"But I don't wish they were here," Laurie said.

"Me, neither."

"This would be a different trip with husbands or children."

"Definitely."

"I like it just the way it is."

"Me, too. A little head soaking is good for the soul."

Laurie laughed before saying one simple word, "More." With that, we went back under into the alternate universe of motion and color and calm.

For a long time, Laurie and I paddled side by side just

below the surface of the water, taking steady breaths in and out of our snorkels on our journey into the submerged universe of tiny miracles. My dearest objective was to get one of the little fish to come to me, but every tactic I tried with my out-stretched hand failed. If we went snorkeling again, I'd definitely bring some peas.

The sun on my back felt hot. Too hot. I knew it would be wise to go back and apply more sunscreen on my pale skin. But I didn't want to ever leave this other world. I didn't want the gentle, rocking sensation that was soothing something deep within me to cease. I was sure Laurie was experiencing the same comfort.

As we stretched out across the saltwater sky of this sequestered universe, I told God I thought He was amazing. From His imagination came all this intriguing variety. Such color and graceful movement. Such exotic terrain.

You spoke and all this came to be.

When we finally floated our way to shore, we couldn't stop effusing about the world we had just peeked into. The older couple beside us seemed entertained by our descriptions.

"Where's our sushi, then?" the man teased.

"They were too small," Laurie said.

"No, they were too amazing," I said. "If you go out there and meet them face-to-face, you'll see what I'm talking about. You could never find it in your being to eat one of those little creatures."

"What do you think, Rosie?" the man asked his wife.

"Should we rent some of those masks and visit the fish?"

"Why not?"

"Here." Laurie held out her mask. "You can borrow ours. I'm sure they have a way of sanitizing the snorkels at the rental shack."

"Oh, I don't think I could manage that gizmo," the woman said. "I'll just try the goggles."

As the white-haired couple tottered to the water, I patted my face and arms dry and lowered my dripping body onto my towel. I couldn't stop talking about the fish.

"I loved the ones that were about the size of my hand."

"Which ones?" Laurie asked.

"The really bright ones that looked like they were painted by a group of Brownies who were trying to outdo each other for their fun-with-color merit badge."

"Hope."

"What? What are you smiling about?"

"You, Hope. You are so full of life. Everything is amazing to you. I love it. I love being around you."

"The feeling is mutual, you know."

Twenty

By the time we got back on the road, it was nearly five o'clock and we were both starving. We drove up along the coast and stopped at the first drive-through we spotted. Eagerly we ordered big burgers with no onions and thick milk shakes. I was a happy mama.

"I was looking at the tour book on the beach earlier," Laurie said, as she steered with one hand and held her vanilla shake with the other. "I thought we could drive around the whole island today, but it's getting pretty late, and the sun will be going down soon. I don't know about you, but I wouldn't mind getting the sand out of my bathing suit before I sit much longer."

"Do you want to turn around and go back the way we came?" I asked.

"Isn't there a highway that goes over the hill and back into Honolulu?"

I had a look at the map. "It's the Pali Highway. We can cut over to Honolulu on that, and it should save us some time."

"And," Laurie said with a sparkle in her voice, "it will get us on a road that has some personality."

I soon found out what Laurie meant by "personality." The Pali Highway was by no means a country road, but as soon as it turned uphill, the terrain changed. The air cooled. The light began to fade. This was a rain forest. Shades of lush green dominated the scene.

"You would think we were on a different planet all of a sudden," Laurie said. "And where are all these people going?"

"Home from the beach?" I suggested.

"I can't believe there's so much traffic on this island. Hope, what do you think of keeping the car another day and driving up to the North Shore tomorrow?"

"Fine with me. You want to find a place to drive without traffic, don't you?"

"How did you know?"

"Just a wild guess."

"I'm ready to put the top back up." Laurie pulled off to the side of the road. We were both in our damp bathing suits and wrapped in wet, sandy towels. The heater was on, but all it was doing was frying the tops of our bare feet. Laurie pushed a button, and when the top connected with the windshield, we snapped a few levers.

"Too easy," she said, turning on her blinker and making a jet-blast merge back into the flow of traffic. We rumbled our way along the beautiful Pali Highway as the day closed its eyes. We were being sent into that place of mystery and imagination where every movement in the shadows is as murky as the shapes one perceives on the inside of the eyelids when trying to fall asleep in the middle of the day.

"This island has many different moods, don't you think?"

Laurie agreed.

Coming down the other side of Pali, we were stunned by the millions of night-lights that had come on all over Honolulu. The one night-light that reduced all the others to firefly flickers was the lopsided moon. It hung from the heavens on invisible wires like a backward, tipsy letter *C*. We hadn't really noticed it before tonight; apparently much of its robust beauty had been hidden by the tall buildings that rose out of the volcanic foundation and defined the Honolulu skyline.

"*La bella luna,*" Laurie exclaimed with a smooth Italian accent. "Look at that beautiful moon!"

I grinned, aware that Laurie was now the one who was amazed and filled with appreciation for God's incredible creation.

"Look at the faint colors in the sky," she said.

The sun had set, yet the sky maintained a periwinkle blue tint that separated the sky blue from the turquoise blue of the vast ocean. A thin vanilla haze shrouded the moon, as if the shy keeper of the night was veiled in gossamer to hide its face from the glory of all that lay stretched out before us.

"This is a gorgeous island. I don't care what anyone says.

It's beautiful. I can see why so many people live here." Laurie paused, and then glancing at me, she added, "Maybe Gabe and I should move here."

I couldn't tell if she was serious or not. Just in case she was, I added, "If you do, I promise I'll come visit you often."

Twenty-One

Sunday, Laurie and I agreed, had been a stellar day in every way. As we turned the car keys over to the bellman at the entrance of our hotel, we discussed how we couldn't have planned a more perfect day.

Then we walked into the lobby, and the tide turned.

Our hotel was filled with people. All of them wore bright yellow laminated name tags. A reception was in full swing out at the pool with live music echoing through the hotel. We wove our way through clusters of conventioneers and waited for the elevator. A particularly loud pair of men joined us, holding plastic drink cups and laughing over a less than honorable joke.

"Pardon me," another man said, stepping toward us. "Are these gentlemen bothering you young ladies?"

Laurie ignored him.

I offered a slight nod because, at first, I thought he was

with hotel security. Then I noticed he was holding a plastic cup. The faint scent of tiki punch wafted in the air.

One of the guys said to the other, "These hotshots from Division Twelve think they can come here and kick some serious—"

Just then the elevator door opened, and Laurie and I hurried inside, claiming the front corner by the control buttons.

"We're gonna dominate this year!" Tiki man called out, as the doors closed with Laurie and me in the elevator with the two guys.

"So, what division are you two in?" one of the men asked us. It sounded about as skanky as if he had said, "So, ya come here often?"

Laurie ignored them.

I was about to state firmly that we were not with their convention, whatever their convention was, and therefore we had no interest in divisions of any sort. But the elevator stopped unexpectedly on the second floor. It wasn't our floor, but Laurie gave me a stern look and stepped out. I followed her.

"See you girls later," one of the guys called out as the door closed.

"Come on." Laurie took my beach bag from me so that my hands were free. "We're taking the stairs. I didn't want them to know which floor we're staying on."

"Oh, right, like they were trying to pick us up."

"Hope, it's not worth trying to reason with an inebriated

person. I've been to enough art-world dinners with Gabe to know that. Come on."

I followed her to the stairwell and took the steps, feeling as if I had fifty-pound weights tied to each ankle. Laurie scooted up the stairs as if she were trying out for an exercise video.

"I'm coming, I'm coming!" I called out.

I made it all the way to the eighth floor. Breathing hard, I stopped outside the stairwell door. "Isn't it the big bad wolves who are supposed to do all the huffing and puffing?"

"In fairy tales, I suppose."

"Next time, we take the elevator and make the wolves take the stairs."

"I hope there isn't a next time." Laurie led the way down the hall to our room.

She showered while I went out on the lanai to cool off. I called Darren, planning to tell him about Juliette's grave and the Hawaiian hymn that went inside me and the zippy little silvery fish that I tried to touch while snorkeling.

However, Darren started the conversation with, "We stayed home from church today. Blake has a cough, and the other two said they felt like they were coming down with something. It snowed six inches last night; did I tell you that?"

Snow. What a foreign concept. The only white stuff I could relate to was the six inches of white sand granules that still lined the inside of my bathing suit.

"Is it cold?" I knew the question was ridiculous the instant I asked, but I was standing outside, barefoot and wearing shorts and Darren's big, white shirt. And I was perspiring like crazy.

"It's freezing," Darren said. "How's the weather there?"

I remembered Laurie's rules for calling home and talking to husbands. What was number two? Something about sounding a little tired and a little sad?

"It's been okay. Friday it rained all day. Just poured. Our luau was canceled because of it." I added a little sigh.

"That's too bad."

"Yeah."

I was thinking of how ridiculous it was to pay roaming fees to Connecticut to talk with my husband about the weather. I knew once I got home I'd be able to give him all the details face-to-face, so I cut to rule number three and gave the ol' one-two closing punch in the right order. "I miss you, Darren. I love you so much."

"I love you and miss you, too. All of us do. It's not the same around here without you."

"I'll be home in a few days. Tell the boys I love them."

"I will. Give Emilee a pat from her daddy."

"Okay. I'm patting her right now."

"Hey," Darren said. "I just looked at the clock. It's after midnight here."

"I know; it's getting late. I should let you go."

"No, I'm saying it's after midnight…so it's your birthday. At least it is here. Happy birthday, Hope."

"Thanks."

I hung up feeling stunned. I wasn't ready to be forty. I went inside, sat on the edge of the bed, and contemplated how I happened to get so old so fast.

Laurie stepped out of the bathroom, her skin glowing with the coconut-scented after-sun lotion she used.

"Are you okay?" she asked.

"I called Darren."

"Uh-oh. Another dish soap crisis?"

"No. He told me, 'Happy birthday.' In Connecticut I'm already forty."

"Well, then it's a good thing you're not in Connecticut right now, isn't it? Because you're still thirty-nine in our time zone."

I offered a weak smile.

"I know." Laurie perched on the edge of my bed. "Here's an idea. Let's celebrate by catching a plane to Hong Kong."

"What are you saying? Traveling east is going to keep me young?"

"Sure. If we time it right and catch the right flights, we could keep you thirty-nine almost all the way to Helsinki!"

"Nice try, Laurie. Thanks. *E* for effort."

"You are seriously bummed about this, aren't you?"

"I didn't think I would be. It sort of sneaks up on you, doesn't it?"

Laurie nodded sympathetically. "It's not so bad once you get to the other side. I know a woman who had never surfed a day in her life. After she turned forty, she was out there surfing like Gidget with the big boys."

Laurie had no way of knowing that her successful attempt to shoot the curl with Moondoggie carried a sting of regret for me since I wasn't even able to try.

"I'm okay," I said. "Just tired. It'll feel good to get this sand out of my shorts."

"Has the time come for some serious Oreos and Reese's Pieces? You say the word, Hope, and I will brave all twelve divisions of those big bad wolves in the elevator, if you want a little comfort food."

I laughed, but it sounded shallow. "No, I think my tastes are changing. If I'm going to have chocolate, I want the really intense stuff."

"I know what you mean. Dark chocolate truffles with cappuccino filling. Now that's something I always have room for. Two little bites, and I'm satisfied for the rest of the day. Of course, those two bites probably pack as many calories as I'd end up having in a stack of Oreos, but I'm convinced that dark chocolate truffles will cure anything. They are definitely my new take-two-and-call-me-in-the-morning favorite."

"Chocolate sounds pretty divine right about now."

"Why don't I call room service and see what they can bring up to us?" Laurie walked over to the desk and opened the padded binder to the room service dessert menu. She read off the list of delectables.

I stopped her when she got to the cookie list. "That's what I'd like: a couple of those white chocolate macadamia nut cookies. And a glass of milk."

"Good choice for a bedtime snack." Laurie picked up the phone.

"Yeah, my last meal as a thirty-nine-year-old," I said glumly. "Tell me when it arrives. I'll be in the shower."

I took my time under the refreshing spray, shaving my legs and conditioning my short hair twice. I asked myself why it seemed like such a big deal to turn forty. All along I had been saying that it wouldn't bother me. Laurie and I were here to celebrate, not mope.

Exiting the bathroom with a puff of steam following me like an albino parrot on my shoulder, I glanced around for the milk and cookies tray.

"Not here yet?"

"No, they said they had a backup of orders in the kitchen, and it would take longer than usual."

I stopped and listened. "What is that noise?"

Laurie motioned to the wall behind our headboards. "Our neighbors are having a party in their room."

"You don't suppose it's the Division Twelve guys, do you? I hope they're not going to be at it with the loud music all night." I listened again to the peals of laughter and loud voices. "How many people do you think they have in there?"

"Too many. If it doesn't quiet down by the time we go to bed, I'm calling hotel security."

Lowering myself into the chair at the desk, I said, "What happened to our cozy little hideaway hotel?"

"They booked a large convention. I know the objective is

to fill all the rooms, but it does change the feel of the whole hotel, doesn't it?"

"It will probably be bedlam around the pool and at the beach tomorrow. We had a hard time finding available lounge chairs the first day we were out by the pool. Imagine what it will be like with so many people here now."

"Maybe they'll be in meetings all day," Laurie suggested.

"Or in bed with a hangover."

"It's a good thing we kept the car another day. We can find a less crowded place to spend your birthday."

The cookies and milk showed up. I got comfy on my bed and began my dunking ritual. I tried to soak each chunk of cookie to just the right degree of sogginess before pulling it from the glass of milk and getting it to my mouth without dribbling.

"You're pretty good at that," Laurie said, taking nibbles of her cookie.

"Thanks."

"It's kind of like my little-known skill of roasting a marshmallow to a nice toasty brown without catching it on fire."

Just then the rowdy neighbors hit our common wall with such a thump that Laurie and I involuntarily ducked.

"That's it. I'm calling the front desk. This is ridiculous."

I scooted closer to the center of my bed, away from the large pictures hanging over the headboard and tried to continue my cookie-dunking ceremony with a little dignity.

"It's like in *Breakfast at Tiffany's,*" Laurie said. "Do you remember the wild party Holly Golightly had in her tiny New York apartment?"

I shook my head.

"Mickey Rooney was the neighbor who ratted on them, and Audrey Hepburn had to sneak out on the fire escape wearing a dress."

"Oh."

"I can tell you, I'm not waiting until women from next door start using our lanai as their fire escape and try to sneak out—Hello? Yes, I'd like to speak to the manager, please."

Within three minutes she seemed to have solved the problem because she hung up and gave me one of her goofy, lipless grins. "Guess what?"

"Surprise me." I lowered another chunk of cookie into my glass of milk.

"We can move to a different hotel."

"Tonight?"

"No, tomorrow morning. The other hotel is part of this chain, but they don't have any conventions going on so they have lots of empty rooms. It's another Kalamela something."

Plop. I lost the last bite of my cookie into the deep white.

"Not the Kalamela Mauka. Tell me you didn't switch us to the Kalamela Mauka. It's not four blocks from here, is it? With a one-eyed dental assistant and a drooping ficus?"

"No, this hotel is half an hour away."

"You're positive they didn't say a half a *mile* away?"

"No, he definitely said half an hour away in a less congested part of the island. It has a private lagoon."

"It may have a private lagoon, but what is the hotel like? What is it rated?"

"I think it's a five-star. He said it was built less than a year ago. That's why they aren't fully booked. People don't know about it."

"Is our room rate going up a lot?"

"That's the best part. When I complained about our noisy neighbors, he apologized for the inconvenience and said we could switch hotels and keep the same rate."

"You just said *if* we switched hotels. It's not a done deal, then?"

"Of course not. Hope, I wouldn't change reservations without talking it over with you. We can stay here if we want. Or we can change. At least we have an option. And the other hotel has a complete spa, which I found out is something this hotel is sadly lacking because I was trying to set up a surprise pedicure for your birthday."

A loud bang against our wall jolted the picture above my bed so that it tilted to the left. I looked back at Laurie. "Private lagoon, huh?"

She nodded. "And don't forget the complete spa."

"I'm in."

Then, thinking I was so clever, I added, "Go ahead. Make reservations for two for breakfast at Tiffany's."

"No, Hope, you see, you don't actually eat at Tiffany's. In the movie…it's…oh, never mind."

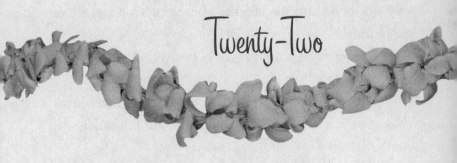

Twenty-Two

I know they say that nothing happens overnight, but I think getting old is the exception. I woke up feeling old. I felt achy and stiff and grouchy. Laurie said it was all the swimming from the day before.

She had her bags packed and was ready to make the hotel switch before I was out of bed.

"Take your time," she said. "It's your birthday. You can do whatever you want. How about if I go down to the espresso cart and get us some lattes?"

"Make mine a jumbo," I said. "With all the fat and all the caffeine and all the whatever else they can throw in. Marshmallows, if they have them."

"How about chocolate? I'll get you a nice big, fat brevé mocha latte with an extra shot. It'll perk you right up."

"Whatever." I felt as if I'd taken a dangerous leap to the

wild side by starting the first day of my forties without a nice cuppa tea.

"I'll make a coffee drinker out of you yet," she said on her way out the door.

"Yeah," I spoofed to the now-empty room. "Like there's even any room for coffee after you put all that fun stuff in the cup!"

I rolled over and thought, *It's good to be under Laurie's wing on such a day as this.*

Bumping around the room, I packed my things. All my clothes seemed to have expanded or somehow billowed with the flowing breezes they had been in, because I couldn't get everything compact enough to close the suitcase. I borrowed the plastic bag in the closet that was marked for dry cleaning.

Laurie returned with two croissants, a plastic container of fruit salad, and a coffee-scented beverage. She also had a fresh-from-the-gift-shop purple orchid lei over her arm, which she graciously placed over my head.

"Aloha, birthday girl."

I sat there, on the edge of the bed, in my pajamas with a purple lei around my neck and a foaming latte in my hand. I felt like a clown posing for an ad for a circus cruise to the Caribbean.

"Try putting a little pineapple in your system," Laurie suggested. "If the pineapple doesn't do it for you, go directly to the mango."

I popped a pineapple chunk in my mouth and slowly sucked on it as if it were a throat lozenge.

"The shock of turning forty will wear off in a few days. Trust me."

"I'm so glad we came here," I said. "I never expected to slide into such an emotional slump."

"I'm glad we came, too. We're going to have a wonderful day. You'll see."

Laurie's enthusiasm made her sparkle. It was a challenge, though, to coax my spirits to rise to the same level as hers. She seemed to understand my quietness.

In the same way that I had wholeheartedly defended Gabriel Giordani's reputation while Laurie quietly examined statues of barnacle-encrusted blue whales at the art gallery, Laurie now went after this day with enough fervor and elation for both of us. I was free to float through it any way I could.

I soon discovered that Laurie's idea of wholehearted fervor and elation was to slip into our red-hot convertible and drive like a female mud wrestler ex-con out on parole.

Ten minutes out of Honolulu, the freeway cleared of morning traffic. Few motorists seemed interested in going in our direction. The road was wide open, with three lanes of straight black asphalt, daring Laurinda Sue to punch it.

And she did.

I tried to think it was fun. I really did. I grinned from ear to ear, when she was looking. When she wasn't looking, I gripped the door handle, gritted my teeth, glued my feet to the floorboard, and groaned so deep inside that Emilee woke up. I do believe those next twenty minutes zooming down the freeway opened up a whole new avenue of my prayer life.

I admit that I drive like a soccer mom in our family van that has more than 156,000 miles on it. I also admit that the roads I travel every day are never void of other cars, making it impossible to drive fast.

Laurie, however, was weaned on wine country roads, and she knew how to take every curve with control and ease. It was too bad I couldn't relax and see the fun in this blast of bliss. Laurie was certainly having a grand time. I kept checking the side mirror to see if a policeman had yet been informed of our red-hot bullet mobile, shooting down the highway.

Taking the designated off-ramp, Laurie then drove sedately down a wide thoroughfare that headed toward the ocean. We saw the large hotel ahead of us and knew it must be the Kalamela Lagoon. In stark contrast to the hotels lining the beach at Waikiki, this one stood all by itself. Construction was in progress on buildings on both sides of the hotel, but for now, this gem dominated.

"Swanky," I said, as we pulled under the wide portico and were greeted by four bellmen in white double-breasted blazers and white shorts.

We entered the open-air lobby, and the heady fragrance of tuberose floated our direction. I caught my reflection in a large oval mirror by the bellman's desk. It was all I could do to keep from laughing aloud. The wind had thoroughly styled my hair on the way to the hotel. Instead of my favorite "swims with dolphins" coiffure, today's selection looked more like "sleeps with typhoons." I ran my fingers through the short strands and tried to tame it to a reasonable fluff.

Laurie went to the front desk, and I stopped at a round table in the center of the lobby to sniff the tuberose and marvel at the most gigantic bouquet of tropical flowers I had ever seen. The stalks of pink ginger must have been at least four feet tall. I couldn't count all the open buds of heady, white tuberose dotting the dozen or more long, green stems.

Look what You made, God. Look at all these colors and shapes! And the fragrance! These flowers would have been beautiful even if You hadn't given them a scent, but that makes them even more magnificent. How gorgeous!

I smiled peacefully for the first time that day. I loved being an audience of one when it came to these little side performances God seemed to be putting on all over this island. I loved discovering the variety of His hidden beauty.

A soft breeze brushed past me, stirring the flowers, releasing their fragrance. In my heart's deepest corner, I felt as if the very Spirit of God was coming close to me, right up to my face, and breathing on me.

Aloha.

My heart beat faster. It wasn't Emilee's little bare-feet tap dance. It was my heart beating with a familiar longing. A longing to come closer to God.

I closed my eyes and drew in the deepest breath I could

swallow. I could taste the nectar from the flowers.

Aloha, I answered back. *I entrust to You, Lord God, the essence of all that I am—all that You made me to be.*

The sweetness of that fragrant moment lingered. I held in my breath, as if I had somehow caught a rare whiff of all that is eternal. I was filled.

Laurie was flabbergasted. "Listen to this," she said, sashaying her way over to me after having checked us in. "We were upgraded to an ocean-view suite because of the inconvenience of having to change hotels, and look what else they gave us." Laurie held out two gift certificates.

I read the wording on the front of them. "Complimentary Spa Selection. What does that mean?"

"That means these little piggies are going *oui, oui, oui* all the way home."

"Our pedicures," I said with a smile.

"Come on. The elevators are over here. We're on the fourth floor."

We found the suite to be three times the size of our luxurious hotel room at the Kalamela Makai and very much to our liking. Neither of us missed the wild red and white hibiscus decor. The kitsch had been fun the first few days, but then we kept looking for a dimmer switch to tone down the lights and realized it wasn't the light but the color we wanted to tone down.

The lanai was almost half the size of our former hotel room and offered a view of the postcard-perfect, pristine lagoon with its languid azure blue waters and crescent-shaped white sandy beach. A dozen empty padded lounger chairs waited under thatched cabanas that waved their palm fronds at us and seemed to say, "Pick me! Pick me!"

I couldn't wait to saunter down to the beach and begin the difficult task of selecting just one of them for an afternoon siesta.

The pool area had to be four times the size of our other hotel's and nearly devoid of patrons. I loved the deep royal blue shade of tile that lined the pool—a round pool, no less. As round as a big, blue moon.

We didn't know what to do first. Schedule our pedicures? Order brunch by the pool? Try out the padded lounge chairs under the cabanas? Or swim in the lagoon? Our bellman said if we went snorkeling in the lagoon, the sea turtles would swim with us.

"What do you suppose is wrong with this place?" I leaned over to more closely examine one of the three potted orchids in our room.

"It's new," Laurie said. "Didn't I tell you? People don't know about it yet."

"Let's not tell them. At least not until after we leave. I can't believe this place. And for the same price as Waikiki!"

Laurie nodded. "It's remote. We can't just walk to a restaurant or gift shop. We're limited to what's on-site."

"That's okay. Besides, we have the car, if we want to go any-where. I'm thinking all I want to do is go down to that lagoon and try out one of those lounge chairs. Either that or get in the water and find one of those sea turtles."

"Whatever the birthday girl wants, the birthday girl gets."

"My wishes are simple: a bottle of sunscreen, a good book, and something tall and iced with a little umbrella to add to my collection."

This time we ordered coconut-papaya blended drinks from the poolside bar and stretched out on a couple of padded loungers under a beach cabana. The winning cabana was the one that was closest to the rest rooms. My choice, naturally.

"Laurie, dahling, what do you suppose women of leisure and unlimited financial means do with their time?"

"You're asking me?"

"I believe I now know the answer to such a question first-hand. They come here and have their nails done and their hair done, and they get undone by the quiet, the sun, and this exquisite, sugar-fine sand."

"We are turning into perfect snoots, I hope you know."

"Oh, I know, dahling." I flipped on my sunglasses and lay with my face toward the glorious sun. "I hope you know that I am now permanently ruined. I will never again be able to live a normal life."

"No more tent camping for you, huh?"

"You won't tell Darren, will you?"

Laurie switched from her snooty accent and said in a lowered voice, "I won't tell him, if you won't tell Gabe that I'm still struggling with the decision to buy the house. I'm open to it.

Not crazy about it. Just open to it."

Laurie's cell phone rang. She looked at the display screen to see where the call was coming from. "That's a little too creepy," she said before pressing the talk button. "Hi! Did you know I was just talking about you?"

I guessed that Laurie might appreciate a little privacy so I rolled over and trotted through the hot sand to the lagoon. The water felt surprisingly warm. Warmer than the water had felt at Waikiki. I wondered about the sea turtle report. Were they really out there? They wouldn't sneak up and nip at my toes, would they?

Let's see, swims with dolphins hair and pedicured by turtles feet. Naw. Doesn't have the same snap to it.

Ha! Turtles. Snap. Ha!

I looked around to see if I had been talking aloud, or if it had all been under my breath. Not that it mattered. But when a woman my age starts entertaining herself so thoroughly, I suppose it's best if she does so in the quiet confines of her own, premenopausal mind.

Twenty-Three

Trucking up to the lagoon rental shack, I checked out two sets of snorkel gear and another towel. For fun, I bought an underwater camera that could attach to my wrist with a rubber loop.

I realized the film I had sent in for developing would be delivered back at the other hotel instead of here. Borrowing the cabana house phone, I called the concierge and made arrangements for the photos to be sent to our new hotel.

Laurie was still on the phone, so I left her snorkel beside her lounge chair, and with flippers on my feet, I flapped down to the shore.

There were many advantages to being among only a handful of guests. First, I didn't feel as if anyone was watching my "creature from the black lagoon" imitation except Laurie; and second, we had left most of our valuables in the room, and it felt safe enough to leave our bags by our chairs since they were in view of where we would be swimming. That made it easy for both of us to go snorkeling at the same time.

With gentle ease I stretched out in the calm, shallow water. Emilee went in first, before the rest of me. She didn't seem to mind because an instant later we were floating. Floating, I decided, was my new hobby. This was divine.

The fins allowed me to move swiftly without much effort on the part of my sore arms. That was a plus.

I headed toward the lagoon's center. We had heard from the bellman that the lagoon was man-made, and the sand had been shipped in from another island to form this ideal corner of paradise. I didn't mind the artificial methods to create such a serene place. The results were fabulous.

I saw a few fish and chased them, trying to coax them to hold still for an underwater photo. Being a little camera shy, they darted away faster than my flippers could propel me toward them. The water was murky, so even though I snapped three pictures, I didn't have high hopes that they would be clear. The fish apparently weren't accustomed to being spied on in this newly formed lagoon and therefore weren't used to smiling for the tourists.

I was content to paddle around, looking right and left for the sea turtles. I expected them to be the size of a half-dollar and floating on the water's surface like tiny green jellyfish. That's why I let out a startled cry through my snorkel when I actually saw one. The friendly green fellow was as big as my largest frying pan and had long, paddle-like arms that propelled him through the water. He came so close I could see his dark button eyes and the folds of wrinkled turtle skin on his extended neck.

He seemed to curiously examine me for a moment before banking to the right and taking off for more interesting sights. I was so engaged in the moment that I didn't think to take a picture. Quickly surfacing, I looked around to see if I could tell where he was going. Another swimmer was coming toward me.

It was Laurie.

"I saw a turtle," I told her, popping the snorkel out of my mouth.

"Where?"

"He went that way. I want to get his picture."

We joined in tandem, kicking and splashing our way in pursuit of the cunning creature. Laurie spotted him first. She tapped my arm and pointed. I could hear her muffled chortle through the water. She motioned for me to follow. We puttered all around the lagoon in pursuit of the not-to-be-bothered sea turtle. Apparently he had gotten his eyeful of me as the tourist du jour, and that was enough for him.

So I took pictures of Laurie instead. At my request, she imitated a sea turtle underwater by stretching out her neck and flapping her arms. She can be a very good sport when she's in a good mood.

I was curious to know if the good mood had anything to do with the conversation she just had with Gabe.

We surfaced, and I asked, "What did Gabe have to say?"

"We're not putting in an offer."

"Really? What happened?" I felt a bit peculiar having this important conversation while treading water with big flippers on our feet and suction-cup circles outlining the path the masks had followed around our eyes. Add bright green snorkels that flapped against our seaweed-style hair every time we moved our heads, and the sum was a situation in which only the best of friends could pay attention to the words that were being said.

"The sellers changed their minds," Laurie said. "They decided to will the house to one of their grown children rather than sell it."

"How does Gabe feel about that?"

"Disappointed, but he said it obviously wasn't the right house or the right time."

"And how do you feel?"

"Relieved and a little angry."

"Angry about what?"

"I'm mad at myself because I spent so much emotional energy trying to fight through this decision. I tried not to bring it up a lot, but you wouldn't believe how much I thought about it our first few days here."

She shook her head, and the snorkel flapped against her ear, looking like a strange gill opening and closing. "I wish I could learn how to have that unforced rhythm of grace when it comes to things like this," she said. "It always turns out fine. Ultimately, God puts all the right pieces in place, but I waste so much time trying to either force things to go the way I want, or I analyze them to death. Why can't I just go with it?"

On Laurie's left side, less than a foot away, two turtles' heads popped out of the water. It was as if turtle number one had gone home to get her best friend and said, "You gotta come see this. A couple of humans are flailing around the lagoon wearing big bug eyes and sucking on giant electric eels!"

"Hold very still," I said, slowly lifting the camera.

"Oh, come on, Hope. I don't need another photo of me with a rainbow shooting out of my head!"

"It's not a rainbow. It's the turtle twins." I snapped the shot before Laurie could turn.

Down went the turtles. On went our masks and snorkels. In went our bodies.

There they were! Turtle one and turtle two. They appeared as fascinated with us as we were with them. Only they could dive deeper than we could and make a faster getaway. For ten minutes, Laurie swished after them as I trailed behind, using poor Emilee Rose as my safety flotation device.

Two minutes into the trek Laurie motioned for me to surrender the camera to her. Of course.

Curiosity satisfied, apparently, the turtle twins took off.

"Maybe they had an appointment at the spa for a manicure or a facial," I told Laurie when we surfaced to catch our breath.

"I have one more shot," Laurie said. "Let me get an underwater picture of you."

Down I went, both hands waving. A silvery gray fish with a

long snout loitered for the longest time in the water between Laurie and me. I hoped he would show up in the picture.

We flippered our way back to the beach and laid ourselves out to dry in the sun like freshly laundered rag dolls, all floppy and loose with matted hair and ridiculously happy grins sewn on our faces.

"Laurie?"

"Hmmm?"

"I don't think I let you finish what you were saying about Gabe and the house and how you felt."

"I was done," she said without opening her eyes.

"Laurie?"

"Hmmm?"

"I think I know what it means to do the hula. You know how you said we needed to come to Hawai'i so we could learn to do the hula? Well, I think you said it back there in the water. We have to learn to just go with it, to live in that unforced rhythm of grace. We listen to the music, or what did Amy call it? Oh yeah, the mele. We listen to the mele, the poetry, the story of our lives, and then we just go with it and express the story as gracefully as we can. Don't you think? That's really what it means to learn to do the hula. At least that's what I think."

No response.

Here I had just made this jubilant birthday speech, and Laurie had fallen asleep. *Ah, well, just go with it.*

I closed my eyes and dreamed of blue—blue water, blue sky, blue moon.

When I woke, I noticed something new on the beach a few yards away. A white tent had been set up on the sand. The breeze was blowing through it, causing the sides to billow gently.

A woman in a white smock was coming toward us. "Aloha. Would either of you like to use our on-the-beach spa?"

I looked at Laurie. She was just beginning to wake up. "What?"

"We can have our pedicures on the beach," I explained. "In the tent over there."

"Now?"

"You don't have to come right now," the woman said. "We will be available to you all afternoon. Let us know how we can be of service to you." She made her way back to the spa tent.

"What do you think?" I asked Laurie. "Pretty decadent, having my first pedicure on the beach."

"Anything for the birthday girl." Laurie sat up in her chair and stretched. "Do they have showers around here? I'm going to rinse off this saltwater residue, and then I'll go with you, if you want. I mean, if you're ready for your birthday pedicure now."

"I'm ready."

We showered and smoothed back our hair, making jokes about how funny we both looked when we first woke up. "That salon technician must have taken one look at the two of us and thought she better come right over and offer their services."

"We might need to order up more than just a pedicure," Laurie said.

"That's true."

Laurie and I entered the cool enclosure. It felt private, yet open enough for the breeze to flow through and for us to view the beauty all around. We announced that we wanted to have pedicures, and the woman in the white coat quickly made a call to the salon and had them deliver the necessary equipment as well as another salon specialist.

Seated in regal luxury, we soaked our feet in a warm, sudsy bath and chatted leisurely as the pedicurists massaged our feet and carefully trimmed our toenails. Fruity beverages, complete with the all-important umbrella, were served to us along with complimentary sushi.

I avoided the sushi.

Laurie loved the sushi. She gave me a rousing speech about how, if I wasn't willing to try something at forty, then I would be less likely to try it at fifty, etcetera. She gave me the whole spiel about not being chicken because we're sisterchicks and how we weren't going home with any regrets for not trying something new.

I finally gave in and took dainty bites, making the appropriate expressions of appreciation. And then I was done. With the sushi and the pedicure. I had tried two new things.

When we returned to our cabana-shaded lounge chairs, Laurie asked me for my conclusions on the experience. Then she said, "Wait. I have to go to the rest room."

"Well, now, that's role reversal."

"Here." She handed me a piece of paper that had the hotel's daily schedule printed on the front. "Write it out, and I'll be back in a jiff."

I had no idea why she asked me to write it out, but I found a pen in the bottom of my bag and had some fun with my review:

#1—Regarding the sushi: I will continue to avoid uncooked fish. Unless they come swimming up to me in underwater social settings. Then I will be the perfect hostess by offering them frozen peas and asking if we might have our picture taken together.

#2—Regarding the pedicure: I will want one every month for the rest of my life, and my husband will never understand. I went with the firecracker red polish because the golden glimmers seem to catch the sunlight. I thought the color might draw attention to my feet, and that's a good thing. Underwater, my sparkling toes might attract uncooked fish. For my thoughts on uncooked fish, see #1.

Unfortunately, Laurie never saw the written version of my comments because of what happened next.

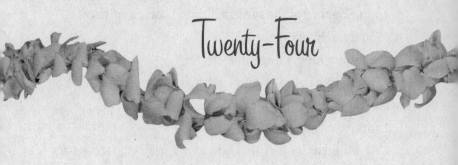

Twenty-Four

That *Laurie*. She didn't really have to go to the bathroom. Her flimsy excuse should have been my clue that she was up to something.

The writing request apparently had been to keep me from watching her as she came traipsing back through the sand with my birthday cake. Or rather, my birthday cookie. She had special-ordered it at a bakery in the mall last Friday when she went shopping.

The white chocolate macadamia nut cookie was the size of a large pizza, and across the top in chocolate frosting was the word *Aloha.*"

"Oh, Laurie, you're so good to me!"

"I try."

"All we need is a couple glasses of milk."

A waiter, whom I hadn't seen approach us, held out a tray with two glasses of milk.

Laurie laughed at the surprised expression on my face.

"You thought of everything."

"Not everything. I forgot the candle."

"That's okay. I already know what my wish is. I thought of it while we were getting our pedicures."

Laurie was all ears.

"My birthday wish is that you and I fetch our sunglasses and drive around until the moon comes out."

"Are you serious?"

I nodded.

"Hope, you were a bundle of nerves the whole way here, and I wasn't going all that fast."

"Are you trying to talk me out of this?"

"No, I'm all for it. You know I'm all for it. Why are you all of a sudden for it?"

"Simple. I am forty years old today, and I never have been behind the wheel of a red convertible."

"Oh, so *you* want to do the driving."

"Yes, of course."

"Well, why didn't you say so?" Laurie stood and collected her belongings. "Come on, Mustang Mama. Let's hit the highway."

I'm not sure why driving our red-hot rental car was such a big deal for me. Maybe it was the closest I would ever get to feeling "cool."

With sweatshirts in hand, we loaded up the car, which the parking attendant had brought around to the hotel's front. For fun, I was wearing my purple orchid birthday lei, even though

I'd had it with me all day at the beach, strung over my lounge chair. It was wilting fast, but I didn't care. It might not be a full garland of hosannas anymore, but it was still a string of yippee.

I had to slide back the seat to create enough room for Emilee between the steering wheel and me. Readjusting the mirrors, I pulled out my sunglasses. "Ready?"

"I was born ready. You know that."

Easing down the wide driveway, I put on my blinker to turn onto the street. No cars could be seen coming in either direction.

"It's all clear," Laurie said with a twinge of impatience in her voice.

"I know. I'm just getting used to how this car feels."

"Sorry," she said. "Don't mind me. I was terrible at teaching the girls to drive. Gabe had to teach all three of them because I picked at every little detail. I'll be quiet."

"You can say whatever you want. I'm not going to guarantee that I'll listen to anything you tell me, but you can say whatever you want."

"Okay, then turn left at the end of this road."

I followed Laurie's directions, and we ended up on the uncrowded freeway. My right foot seemed to respond in direct correlation to the wind in my hair. The faster the ends of my crazy hair danced across my forehead, the heavier my foot became.

Oh yeah! It's a lot different when you're the one behind the wheel!

"Whoo-hoo!" I hollered to the open air.

Laurie laughed. "We're not even going the speed limit yet!"

"I know. But this is fast for me. Just let me enjoy the moment at my own speed, will you?"

Laurie pinched her finger and thumb together and pretended to zip shut her lips.

The wind whipped the ends of my hair. My foot grew heavier.

A small pickup truck zoomed past us with two surfboards hanging out the back. The truck slowed down until we came up alongside it. The two shirtless teenage boys had their arms out the open windows and were pounding the outside of the doors, as if trying to make their beat-up old pony go faster. They sped up and then pulled back, smiling at us and pounding their doors some more.

I realized they weren't trying to make their pony go faster. They were making fun of us because our pony wasn't going as fast as theirs.

The guys sped up. Fragments of their laughter shattered against the windshield and fell on my ears.

"I think that was a challenge," I yelled to Laurie.

She responded with an expression that was half a shrug and half a dare-you-to-do-it gleam.

I have to say that the upside of all Darren's years of coaching is that I've never been intimidated by high school boys who think they're hot stuff. Well, except when I was in high school, and the high school boys really were hot stuff.

"We can take 'em," I said with a snarl.

Laurie did a double take, apparently at the look on my face. Out of the corner of my eye, I saw her grab the side of the passenger's seat. "Punch it!"

I floored our little cherry roadster and flew past the surfer boys in one unbroken straight line. *Zoom!*

There! Ha! What a rush!

In my rearview mirror I saw the defeated driver take his horse from the playing field by turning at the off-ramp.

"We showed them!" I declared with pride.

Laurie's eyes were wide, but she didn't say a word.

As quickly as the spurt of fiendish adrenaline came over me, all sensibilities returned, and I brought our Mustang back to a steady canter. Point proven, I was content to slow way down and take in the scenery.

The one bit of scenery I didn't expect was the bright flashing lights on top of the car that was rapidly coming up behind us.

"Laurie, is that what I think it is?"

"Oh, my word. Hope, pull over."

"We can outrun 'em."

"Hope!"

"Kidding! I'm only kidding. See? I'm pulling over. Nice and slow. Just stay cool. I'll handle this. Where's my purse?"

"In the backseat. Here." Laurie pulled out my wallet. Under her breath she said, "We are so busted."

"Good afternoon." The officer looked in the car at Laurie and me.

I would never readily admit this, but I leaned back a little extra so the officer could see that I was pregnant. Who would give a pregnant woman a speeding ticket?

He adjusted his sunglasses. "You're not on your way to the hospital or anything, are you?"

"No, sir." I felt as if I were eighteen. And here's something else I would never readily admit. I loved it!

"May I see your driver's license?"

"Sure. I'm guessing the registration is in the glove compartment. This is a rental car."

"Oh, really?" he said with a smirk.

Laurie pulled out the rental papers and handed them over with a meek expression. "It's her birthday. She just turned forty today."

"I can see that by the date on her license. Thank you."

I turned to Laurie with a strained expression as if to say, "You don't have to tell the whole world! Let me enjoy feeling like I'm eighteen."

Without anymore comments, witty or otherwise, he started to write on a pad he pulled from his back pocket.

Apparently Laurie was unwilling to let this ticket be issued without a fight. "We were being harassed by some surfers in a truck." Now she was the one who sounded eighteen.

"Harassed, ma'am?"

"Yes. They were going much faster than we were and…"

"Were you trying to pass them?"

"No."

"Trying to get away from them?"

Laurie hesitated.

I answered honestly. "No, we were trying to race them."

He tilted his head and looked at both of us. "You were trying to race them?"

We nodded in innocent unison.

I would have guessed that the uniformed young man was about twenty-five years old. Judging by his build, he probably taught surfing lessons on the weekends. A faint half grin lifted the right corner of his mouth.

"You broke the law," he murmured, returning his attention to the ticket pad.

"Yes, sir. I did." I glanced at Laurie. She was looking down at the floorboard, shaking her head. I was sure she would tell me later I had handled this all wrong by eagerly agreeing to my guilt.

"Here you go." The officer returned my license and the paperwork for the rental car. "Be careful pulling back onto the road and keep to the speed limit from here on out, okay?"

"I will. Thank you."

With a nod, he handed me the ticket and walked back to his squad car.

"What a disaster!" Laurie said. "How much is it for?"

I looked at the slip of paper and burst out laughing.

"What?" Laurie looked over and read what the officer had written on the ticket.

Happy birthday and, hey, don't ever grow up. Aloha.

Laurie laughed with me. "Now, that's grace. I can't believe he didn't pull a 'book 'em, Danno' on you."

I laughed some more. It felt so good. Everything felt good. The sun on my shoulders, the wind in my hair, the birthday gift of grace I had just been given. But especially the feeling that I wasn't old. Forty wasn't the end of the world.

"Let's find a restaurant." I glanced over my shoulder and cautiously pulled onto the road with my blinker on.

"Did you work up an appetite after all that?" Laurie asked.

"No, I laughed so hard I have to…"

"Don't tell me. I can guess. The sign back there said the next off-ramp is a mile and a half up the road."

We pulled off, found a gas station, and then hopped back in with me still at the wheel.

Laurie and I spent the remainder of my birthday driving— the speed limit—singing along with the radio, talking until we were hoarse, and laughing until the moon came out.

It hung there like a golden fishhook in the sky, daring me to jump high enough to get a bite of it. I declined the offer. I'd had enough dares for one day. I didn't need to try for the moon.

I was forty years old, and I was content.

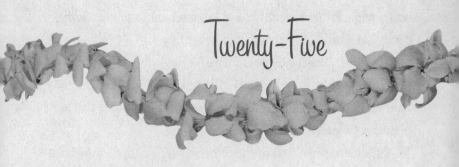

Twenty-Five

$\mathcal{L}$aurie and I had agreed to spend our final day on Oahu driving to the North Shore. Or perhaps I should say, taking turns driving to the North Shore.

We loaded up the car with everything we needed for our romp and were walking out of the hotel when the manager stopped us. "I do apologize, Mrs. Montgomery. If you have a moment, a gentleman is in my office who would like to speak with you."

Laurie and I fell in step like two truants being taken to the principal's office. All I could guess was that the officer had changed his mind and was sitting in there, ready to hand me the speeding ticket I deserved.

The man who was waiting wasn't wearing a police uniform. He looked at us warmly. "Hope Montgomery?"

I stepped forward, but my heart stepped off a cliff. What if something was wrong, really wrong at home? What if this man was a plainclothes detective, and he was here to tell me something that would change my life forever?

"I'm Mr. Takagawa," he said with a slight bow. "I work for the Robert Wilson Galleries. I do apologize for the impolite manner in which I am approaching you, but I was told you are planning to leave the island in the morning."

I nodded, unable to put together a single clue to solve the mystery of why this man wanted to talk to me.

"I wanted to approach you about some of your pictures."

"My pictures?"

Laurie took a step closer and looked at the blown-up images on the manager's desk.

"Your photography is extraordinary. One shot in particular." He reached for a color photo and held it up for us to see. It was a close-up of Kapuna Kalala's hands as she was holding up the lei she had made, offering the fragrance to the Lord. The picture was stunning. The lighting was just right. The detail of the flowers in contrast to her weathered hands was extraordinary. I caught my breath and glanced at Laurie.

"Our gallery would like to purchase this photo and several others. We realize it is highly unconventional for us to be asking this of you, but it is my understanding that the service that developed these photos is preparing to make you an offer, and we hoped to speak with you first."

It was starting to sink in. My name was on the order for developing the film. I called to have the photos forwarded to this hotel. They thought I was the photographer. Laurie looked as stunned as I felt.

"Actually," I said, trying to select my words carefully. "I'm not the photographer. I did take some of the pictures on the rolls, but my friend here is the artist."

He turned his attention to Laurie and held out his hand. "My apologies. I have been presenting myself to the wrong person, it seems. Owen Takagawa."

"I'm…" Laurie hesitated.

"Lali," I said, skipping the Laurinda Sue and the Giordani and going directly to her Hawaiian name. Then remembering that on the calligrapher's sign Sue was *Ku* in Hawaiian, I invented a brand-new name for her right on the spot. "Laliku."

"It is an honor, Laliku," he said, bowing.

Laurie bowed, shooting me a grin out the side of her mouth.

"Laliku is not my legal name," Laurie said delicately. "But I am interested in hearing more about your offer, Mr. Takagawa."

Laurie and I had dressed up a little that morning and had put on makeup because we weren't sure what the day would hold. She sounded professional and looked like she was ready to be all business.

"Perhaps we can discuss the details now, if you are available."

"Yes, now would be fine. Are you by any chance a tea drinker, Mr. Takagawa?" Laurie followed the nodding gentleman out the door and shot me a look that said, "Don't leave me now!"

For the next hour and a half, we had a wonderful conversation with the shrewd businessman. Neither Laurie's last name nor her connection to the art world was part of the discussion.

I used all the correct tea terminology, which pleased Mr. Takagawa, and offered my diplomatic face gestures to Laurie when it came to the business questions. I had learned enough while opening the Ladybug to know that you never sign anything in such a meeting, no matter how persuasive the presenter is. I also suggested to Laurie that she might want her lawyer to look over the documents, and that seemed to jolt her back to the present.

Mr. Takagawa left us sitting in the open-air lobby with his paperwork in a tidy stack. Laurie drew in a deep breath. "Wow."

"Yeah, wow. Look at this picture again, Laurie. You captured it all. Exactly. 'The Fragrant Offering.'"

"That's a perfect title for it. I want to make sure that Kapuna Kalala gets a copy. Thank you, Hope. Really. Thanks for everything."

"Hey, I told you I'd be the midwife, if you needed me."

"I just didn't know you were going to induce labor."

"With those 259-pounders, you have to do whatever it takes."

Laurie smiled. "By the way, where did the *Laliku* come from?"

"Laurie and Sue. It seemed like a good idea at the time. You can change it, of course, but I knew you wanted to avoid the Giordani connection. Sorry if I went too far with it."

"No, I appreciate it. You're quick on your feet, Hope. You saved the day. Seriously."

"We have more of this day to save." I nodded toward the great outside that had been patiently waiting for us to come out and play. "What do you want to do?"

"Let's scream on up to the North Shore, have a look around, and find a place to eat dinner on the beach."

"Sounds perfect."

Laurie drove with a light air about her and a light foot. Being "discovered" seemed to settle on her slowly.

"You know what I just thought?" I said. "We haven't seen the rest of the photos. Did the developing company send them over to the hotel or just selected shots to art dealers?"

"Call the hotel," Laurie said, tossing me her phone. "See if they got them."

"They did," I reported a few minutes later. "They're holding the package for us at the front desk. I can't wait to see the rest."

Laurie saw a sign advertising locally grown Kona coffee for sale and pulled off the road. We parked in the gravel parking area, and I waited in the car while she ventured over to the small wooden stand and bought six bags of the pure Kona coffee.

In the sky above us skittered a fleet of overly ambitious clouds, all determined to block the sun. The temperature cooled.

"Sail on," I told the clouds. "No raindrops, please. Not on our last day."

We cruised past a field of pineapples and came to a crossroad that would take us through several small surf towns along the North Shore.

"Do you want to drive?" Laurie asked. "I'm ready to take some pictures."

"Feeling inspired?"

"I guess I am. I still can't believe it."

We switched places in the car, and as Laurie used up her last four rolls of film, I could tell she was internalizing and analyzing everything that had come her way that morning. Leaving her to contemplate and snap away in peace, I kept our little red tomato cruising along the narrow North Shore road at a slow pace. I loved the calmness in the air.

This part of the island was a stark contrast to the Honolulu district. Many of the houses we passed looked as if they had changed little in the past fifty years. Most of them had nicely trimmed lawns. Large stalks of ginger grew like Roman candles shooting out of large clumps of overgrown bushes. Some of the houses were on stilts. Others were flanked by banana trees that were laden with bunches of the short, green, fingerlike fruit hanging within easy reach.

We drove for a long time, taking it all in. On our left side, white-crested waves dashed toward the shore with great force as the wind sculptured a swift curl of spray across their broad foreheads. The sound of them hitting the rocks was thunderous. We didn't stop to watch the many surfers take on the huge swells because parking was impossible.

On the way back, we stopped at a shop that had surf-boards lined up out front. For each of my boys, I bought a key chain with a small wooden surfboard that had the words *North Shore* hand-painted on it.

"Try this." Laurie squirted a blob of fragrant white lotion into my open hand. The scent reminded me of Kapuna Kalala and the tuberose leis. I bought two bottles, so that whenever I felt a little glum at home, I could rub some on my hands and instantly be transported back to this wonderful place.

Returning to the hotel, we picked up the packet of devel-oped photos and told ourselves we wouldn't look at them until we sat down to dinner. Then the debate began over where to eat.

I'm happy with what we decided in the end. We ate on the nearly empty beach in front of our hotel, all dressed up, bare-foot, and wearing fresh pikake leis that Mr. Takagawa had sent over for us with a kind note.

I settled into the warm, sugar-white sand. "You do promise to help me get up, don't you?"

"Yes. And if I need help, I'll find us a suitable cabana boy."

We laughed and turned our attention to our grilled teriyaki ahi ahi tuna with up-country green beans and jasmine rice, which the restaurant had graciously prepared for us.

"What an amazing trip this has been," Laurie said.

I savored each bite as Laurie reviewed a few of the high-lights. Reaching over, she comfortably patted my round mama belly. "And you, Miss Emilee Rose, have been a delightful stow-away."

The graceful, ancient sun shed her translucent garments that were spun from the softest pink clouds and slowly lowered herself into the great Pacific bathtub, pausing long enough to turn toward us and catch her own shimmering, golden reflection in the azure waters of our lagoon.

"Incredible! Look what You made, God! Wow!" Laurie stood to take the very last pictures of the breathtaking sunset. "I'm starting to sound like you, Hope."

"That's okay. I'm starting to drive like you."

"Not a bad trade-off, I'd say."

"Ready for the pictures before all the light goes?" I reached for the package and made sure my fingers were clean enough to touch them.

"I was born ready," Laurie said.

"You know what? I believe you were. You were born for this."

"Hope, you said the other day that my ability to create this art is a gift God gave me."

"It is."

"Do you remember what Amy told us about the hula? How the objective of the dancer is to gracefully interpret the story that's coming through the music?"

"Yes."

"Well, every life is a story, like Kapuna Kalala said. The artist simply expresses the truth and beauty of that story.

When I think of it that way, it takes the pressure off me some-how. All I have to do is…I don't know how to say it…"

"Go with it," I suggested.

"That's it. Just go with it. The whole unforced-rhythm-of-grace thing. And you know what? I can do that. I can interpret the story because…I'm an artist."

"Wow, Laurie. You said it aloud. Yes! You are an artist. And now you have an opportunity to use that art in a significant way."

Laurie started to leak. Just a little. "You want to know a secret? This is what I wished for on my birthday. I just realized that God granted me my wish."

She started to seriously leak. I started to slush. She moved on to squeaking, and I let loose with the gushing. We were a mess.

"We're going to have to go up by the light around the pool so we can see these," Laurie said, after I'd used up every one of our napkins and was dabbing my final tears with the edge of my sleeve.

Sitting together on a chaise lounge by the pool, Laurie and I went through the pictures. Our heads were bent over the same frame, even though I had ordered doubles of everything.

"Oh, this one has to go," I said. "No way." It was a prepos-terous shot of me receiving a little more than a helping hand on the catamaran.

Laurie grabbed it and busted up. "Gotta love that zoom feature, dolphin girl."

The surf pictures were great fun. It was easy to see the Chihuahua in one of the close-ups, and the shot of Laurie carrying her board back to the surf shop was pure Gidget-gold.

"And what exactly is this one supposed to be?" Laurie pulled out the eagerly anticipated rainbow shot.

I laughed hard. The angle was perfect. "That's you. With a rainbow coming out of your nose."

Laurie laughed even harder. "Maybe I should use this for my new publicity shot." She stared at it some more and shook her head. "This is hilarious. Kudos, Hope."

"Hey, I learned all about angles and capturing the moment from you."

"Well, if the teahouse thing doesn't work out, you know, I just might need an assistant."

When the photos were all examined and exclaimed over, Laurie moved to the chaise lounge beside me, where she stretched out in the balmy breeze. We lingered contentedly as soft Hawaiian music lilted through the air. Above us, the stars glimmered in the night sky, reflecting their unimaginable glory in the still water of the perfectly round, blue-moon swimming pool.

I wanted to go in the pool. I wanted to step right in that pool and scoop up all the stars. I wanted to string them together and lift the garland of radiant glory with both hands as an offering to the Artist above. I wanted God to enjoy His creation tonight as much as I had been enjoying it all week.

Quietly rolling off the chaise lounge, I reverently took my

bare feet to the edge of the empty swimming pool. In even measure with the beckoning Hawaiian music, I lowered myself into the shallow end until the warm water was up to my waist. With barely a whisper, I began to move to the strains of the strumming guitar.

"Hope?"

"Yes."

"Are you in the pool?"

"Yes."

"With all your clothes on?"

"I thought that was better than the alternative."

"What are you doing?"

With sublime ease, I drew the music inside of me and moved my arms and legs in a tender expression, interpreting openly all that was in my heart.

"Hope, are you doing the hula?"

"Yes."

A gentle breeze stroked my cheek. "And you know what, Laurie? This is what I wished for on my birthday."

Around me the music swirled, the water cascaded from my arms, as I lifted them toward heaven. The stars were singing. I know they were.

With the smallest of splashes, Laurie paddled over to where I floated in the center of the pool. Giving way to complete abandon and a steady flutter of giggles, Laurie and I brought a gift of laughter, singing ourselves into His presence. Unforced. Flowing with the rhythm of grace.

I realized then that for our fortieth birthdays, Laurie and I had planned this little island theme party. We didn't know it would turn into a surprise party. The surprise was on us when God showed up. We invited Him, of course, but didn't know if He would be too busy to come.

But He came. Even before the party started, He tied pink and orange streamers to the sun and strung a million bright twinkle lights across the night sky. He passed out crazy fringed party hats to all the palm trees and hired a band of dolphins to kick things off. When Laurie and I arrived, He threw garlands of hosannas around our necks. He brought hundreds of gifts and watched our delighted expressions each time the next gift was unwrapped.

And now here He was, dancing with us, drawing us forehead to forehead with Him so He could breathe on us and trust us with His essence, His Spirit, His aloha.

That was the night these two sisterchicks learned to do the hula.

Epilogue

June 3, 2003
Hartford, Connecticut

Emilee Rose arrived on April 13 at 5:35 in the morning.

She came after an intense four hours of labor. I don't remember the final push, but Darren said I called out, "Po-hue-HUE!" and out she came. Our little morning glory.

Emilee weighed eight pounds and twelve ounces, was twenty-one inches long with a round button nose and full cheeks that we think she will grow into. She has absolutely no hair, and she fills me with such wonder every time I look at her. The boys are crazy about her. And Darren…he adores her with a deep tenderness that a daddy can only have for his little girl.

Laurie had a gorgeous lei sent to me at the hospital. It was made from baby pink roses interspersed with fragrant white tuberose. "A garland of hosannas," the card read. "For Emilee Rose from Auntie Laurie with aloha."

I wore it in the hospital. I didn't care if the New England nurses looked at me as if I were strange. Mine was the sweetest smelling room on the floor.

A month before Emilee arrived, Laurie had sent a special gift for the nursery. It was a beautifully framed print of "Fragrant Offering." Darren hung it over the changing table because he thought it was safer there than over the crib. Of course, one of our boys noticed the title of the picture and thought it was funny we put it over the changing table. So we moved it to the dining room, where I can see it from the kitchen.

Last Sunday we had Emilee dedicated at our church in the first service. Gabe and Laurie came and sat in the front row with us. Darren and I went forward with all three of our sons and stood before the pastor at the altar as he blessed our sleeping baby girl.

As we stood there, our pastor read from John 20. The passage referred to the time soon after Christ's resurrection when He appeared in the upper room to His disciples.

"Jesus said to them again, 'Peace to you! As the Father has sent Me, I also send you.' And when He had said this, He breathed on them, and said to them, 'Receive the Holy Spirit.'"

My heart was pounding. Christ breathed on His disciples. It was right there in God's Word. That's why the concept of aloha had seemed so strangely familiar to me.

Emilee opened her eyes at that moment and looked up at me without crying. I drew her close. Going forehead to forehead with her, I whispered, "Aloha." I could feel her baby's breath on my face.

After the service, Laurie and Gabe joined our family and friends for dinner at the Ladybug Tea and Cakes. Sharla had suggested we cater the event at the Ladybug so I wouldn't have a lot of cleanup at my house. She was running the shop with the help of her niece until the end of the summer, and I was making the most of my time off.

"Did you ask your pastor to read that verse?" Laurie asked me while we went through the buffet line together.

"No. Was that wonderful or what? I'm telling you, Laurie, I haven't been the same since that trip."

Gabe leaned over. "That trip was the best thing you two could have ever done."

"It was your clever wife's idea," I said. "Both times."

Gabe smiled. "She hasn't been the same since. Did she tell you the Kalamela Hotel chain is using her 'Fragrant Offering' picture on the cover of all their brochures?"

"Laurie, that's wonderful!"

"I was going to tell you later. I had a large sepia print done, and Gabe painted in the flowers. It's really extraordinary. The second hotel you and I stayed at bought it, and it's going up in their lobby."

I clapped my hands together. "Laurie!"

"I know."

We were interrupted and had to finish the conversation later that evening back at our home. Gabe was sitting in the living room, rocking Emilee while Laurie and I went through my photo album laughing our hearts out.

Darren and Gabe just looked at each other and shrugged.

Laurie and I decided we would start to plan our next sister-chick trip now. If it took us twenty years to pull off the first one, we knew we'd better get a running start.

Before Gabe and Laurie drove back to their hotel, they told us they had a little gift for us in the trunk of their rental car. I put Emilee to bed. Gabe went outside and returned with a gift bag, which he handed to Laurie, and then carried in a large, flat box.

"This is for you, Hope and Darren," Gabe said. "It might appeal more to you, Hope, but we want you to know that you can do whatever you want with it."

I pulled the gift from the box and laid it on the cleared dining room table before tearing back the brown paper wrapping and exposing a thick, dark wood frame.

"Is this koa wood?"

Gabe nodded, obviously pleased that I recognized the value of the now-rare wood.

Darren pulled back the rest of the wrapping, and all my breath escaped me. Gabriel Giordani had given us an original oil painting of the Hawaiian graveyard where the two magnificent plumeria trees stood guard in full bloom. Hidden away on an obscure white marble gravestone was a purple orchid lei.

The color, the depth, the essence of the picture were astounding. It was the most elegant and dramatic piece he had ever painted.

"He used all the pictures I took of you," Laurie explained, when I had no words to respond. "This oil is the only one. Do you understand what I'm saying? We didn't have any prints made."

Darren and I looked at Gabe. He nodded. "It's yours. If you ever want to have lithos made to sell, I'll work with you on it."

"Gabe, this is...," Darren began. "I don't know what to say."

I impulsively threw my arms around Gabe and kissed him soundly on the cheek. "Thank you! It's beautiful! I love it! Thank you, thank you, thank you!"

Darren shrugged. "I guess that about covers it for both of us." He gave Gabe a manly, arm-around-the-shoulder sort of hug. "Thank you."

"You're welcome." Gabe was beaming. I could tell this scene had captured a small corner of his heart.

"One more present," Laurie said.

"You guys!" I protested.

"This is for Emilee Rose." Laurie held out the gift bag. "I bought it at the gift shop at the Kalamela Makai, and I kept it hidden from you the whole trip."

I pulled from the gift bag an itty-bitty, baby-sized grass hula skirt.

"It's adorable!"

"Read the card," Laurie said with a broad grin.

I opened the envelope and read out loud, "For Emilee Rose, our little sisterchick-in-training."

"Oh, Laurie," I said, starting to slush. "You're so good to Emilee and me."

"I try," she squeaked.

Before she could leak or I could gush, we wrapped our arms around each other and started laughing at our familiar line, immersed in the joy of our sweet, sweet friendship that had taken us to a place where we felt the presence of God like never before.

That Laurie. If it hadn't been for her, I wouldn't know a thing about being a sisterchick. And worse than that—if not for Laurie, I might have gone my whole life without ever learning to do the hula.

Log on to www.sisterchicks.com
for updates on Robin's next Sisterchick novel,
coming in November 2004!

Discussion Questions

1. Have you ever done the hula? Details, please!

2. With your friend, have you ever felt the way Hope did when Laurie came to visit and Hope hid behind the curtains wondering what they would talk about?

3. What is it in a friendship that makes two women feel instantly reconnected after years of not seeing each other?

4. Would you have gone in the ocean your first night like the bobbing Betties? Why or why not?

5. How do you see yourself changing as you get older? Are you more adventuresome or less?

6. Is there a maven in your mirror? What sass-and-slash comments has she been feeding you? How do you overcome the negative messages she dishes out?

7. Have you ever rented a convertible? How did it make you feel when you were riding in it? Do you drive like Lead Foot Laurie, Reluctant Hot Rod Hope, or Slowpoke Sally?

8. What is the wildest adventure you and your sisterchick have ever experienced? The most moving?

9. Do you or your sisterchick have a 259-pound baby that's yearning to be born? How can you serve as midwife-encourager for her? What do you wish she would do for you?

10. According to Laurie's definition, are you in a season of beauty, contentment, or dignity? How do you see this concept being played out in your life?

11. Hope rode high on the blessed-art-thou-among-women cloud when she found out she was pregnant with Emilee Rose. If you've been pregnant, how was your experience similar or different from Hope's?

12. When was the last time you were overwhelmed with the beautiful artistry of God's creation? How did you respond?

13. In what ways have you experienced the "unforced rhythms of grace" lately?

Sisterchick *n.*: a friend who shares the deepest wonders of your heart, loves you like a sister, and provides a reality check when you're being a brat.

Helsinki or Bust!
Ohh, yeah...these gals are gone!

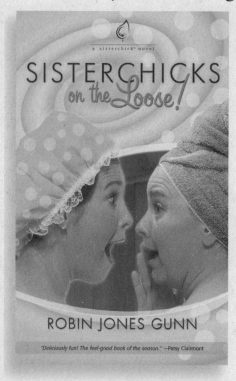

"Deliciously fun! *Sisterchicks on the Loose* is the feel-good book of the season!"

—PATSY CLAIRMONT,
Women of Faith speaker and author of *Stardust on My Pillow*

Meet two very real women who have become unlikely best friends. Sharon is the quiet mother of four; Penny is a former flower child. Their twenty-year friendship takes a surprising leap when Penny plans an impulsive trip to seek out her only living relatives in Finland. The land of reindeer and saunas holds infinite zaniness for these two sisterchicks. They find their hearts filling with a new zest for life and a fresh view of the almighty God who compressed the stars with His hands and flung them across the universe.

ISBN 1-59052-198-6

Join the Sisterchick network at http://www.sisterchicks.com!

Come to Glenbrooke...
"A Quiet Place Where Souls Are Refreshed."

The Glenbrooke Series

#1	Secrets	ISBN 1-57673-420-X
#2	Whispers	ISBN 1-57673-327-0
#3	Echoes	ISBN 1-57673-648-2
#4	Sunsets	ISBN 1-57673-558-3
#5	Clouds	ISBN 1-57673-619-9
#6	Waterfalls	ISBN 1-57673-488-9
#7	Woodlands	ISBN 1-57673-503-6
#8	Wildflowers	ISBN 1-57673-631-8

More Titles from Robin Jones Gunn

TEA AT GLENBROOKE

Snuggle into an overstuffed chair, sip your favorite tea, and journey to Glenbrooke… "a quiet place where souls are refreshed." Written from a tender heart, Robin Jones Gunn transports you to an elegant place of respite, comfort, and serenity—a place you'll never want to leave! Lavishly illustrated by Susan Mink Colclough, look forward to a joyful reading experience that captures the essence of a peaceful place.

ISBN 1-58860-023-8

MOTHERING BY HEART

Focusing upon the special bond between a mother and child, this unique gift book offers lilting poetry, poignant prose, spiritual insights, romantic photographic images, inspiring quotations, and heart-warming journal entries. A delightful companion to women of every age and background celebrating the vast and myriad joys of motherhood!

ISBN 1-57673-914-7

GENTLE PASSAGES

As she shares her own special traditions, Robin Jones Gunn makes the passage into womanhood a tender and joyful celebration—an invitation to a treasured role in God's eyes.

ISBN 1-57673-943